THE HANGMEN OF SAN SABAL

The vicious marshal and the angry posse were hell-bent on stringing up Lake Oliver for a killing he hadn't committed. Admittedly he was an ex-convict, but he was now back on the straight and narrow—so why were the robbery and death of a banker being blamed on him? Oliver had to slip through the fingers of the posse and find out, he needed to trap the real culprit. Although he was wounded, he was aided by pretty rancher Julie Carr, and he might just have a chance of escaping the clutches of the hangmen.

THE HANGMEN OF SAN SABAL

Ray Hogan

GUNSMOKE

This hardback edition 2005
by BBC Audiobooks Ltd
by arrangement with
Golden West Literary Agency

ISBN 1 4056 8020 2

British Library Cataloguing in Publication Data available.

Printed and bound in Great Britain by
Antony Rowe Ltd., Chippenham, Wiltshire

Chapter ONE

Every man, Lake Oliver remembered being told, had the right to one big mistake in his life, and he reckoned he'd used up that privilege. Important thing now was not to make a second one; a man was a fool to trip himself up twice.

Lake had no intention of letting it happen again. Oh, he'd undoubtedly pull off a hatful of stupid boners before he was carted off to the graveyard, being only a few months shy of twenty-five, but they'd be the usual minor things that a fellow got himself crossways with, and not the kind that would put him behind bars.

That's what he'd been through—a solid year behind bars. Twelve long months. Three hundred and sixty-five monotonous, everlasting days. It seemed their slow procession would never end. But he admitted he had it coming to him; he had been there behind those towering brick walls for all that time not because he wasn't guilty but for the simple reason he'd let himself get slicked into something without giving it proper thought—a stage-coach robbery.

Oliver groaned irritably, mopped at the sweat on his forehead, and stared out over the vast, grass-covered New Mexico flat spreading before him. He must have really been liquored up that night in Denver when he'd agreed to throw in with those two newly acquired friends he'd met in the Buckhorn Saloon; and drunker yet when he rode off with them to stop the stage on the Cheyenne road.

He guessed, too, it was just plain dumb, for it had cost him a year in prison—a year of his life. But it was all behind him now and that's where it would stay. It was the old straight and narrow for Lake Oliver from here on. Sure, it would be hard. He was a marked man. He knew that, and he accepted the fact as part of the penalty he must pay for his transgression. However, there was one thing certain —he'd not give the law any reason to come looking for him again.

He'd been lucky in one way. There'd been a job waiting for him when he walked through the big stone gate at the penitentiary. It had been a short-duration deal, to be sure, but he'd made good money. The prison warden, ranching on the side, and learning of Lake's horsebreaking ability, had hired him upon release to tame a herd of mustangs his riders had brought in. At two dollars a head Lake had done well, now had himself a small stake.

Then the warden, evidently seeing in him the makings of a good man if given the chance, had gone further and obtained for him a job on a ranch in southeast Arizona. It wasn't much of a job, just a regular cowhand, but it was a new start and it suited Lake Oliver just fine.

A spread of his own was what he wanted. He'd dreamed of it all during the months of confinement, had actually thought of it even before but never very seriously. Now it was set firmly in his mind; he'd have that ranch.

As soon as he was settled on his new job he'd look around, find the land he'd need, and get his hands on it. Then, as fast as he could, he'd start stocking it with Mexican cattle. Steers were cheap on the other side of the border, he'd heard, and if he was fortunate to find land close to the line, all the better.

It might take three or four years before he'd be in a position to shove off on his own, but that wouldn't matter. Important thing was that he'd eventually have his own place; he'd be working for himself and every drop of sweat and pound of labor he put into it would be to his own advantage, not someone else's. Then, with luck and a few more years, he'd have himself a real layout—one with hired hands, a fair-sized herd, a good house and all.

Oliver grinned at his own daydreaming. But it could come to pass. Hell, most ranchers got started that way; a few cows and a piece of land, hard work, and then one day there it was—a big, important spread. It had happened to other men; there was no reason it couldn't come true for him if he worked hard and kept his nose clean.

He pulled off his hat, once more swiped at the sweat on his forehead. The long-legged bay he was forking—one of the mustangs he'd broken for the warden and later purchased as his own—was moving along steadily, easily, showing no signs of tiring despite the fact he'd been going since well before daylight. The gelding was an exceptional horse; he'd realized that when he'd broken him to the saddle. . . . A horse with a lot of bottom, his pa would have said.

Lake stirred, shifted his weight on the worn hull he'd bought secondhand from one of the warden's punchers. Maybe the bay wasn't tiring but he sure as hell was—tired of the trail, tired of riding, of eating his own grub and sleeping on the ground. He'd been hoping to see a town where he could put up for the night, but so far there'd been none to appear on the high plains. The last settlement had been a small Mexican village and he'd ridden through it too early to stop, even if it had offered accommodations.

Replacing his headgear, he cut in behind a low juniper, halted in its scant shade. Swinging off the saddle, he grunted when his heels hit the solid ground and the ache in his leg muscles began to ease; it was good to come off the leather. . . . There ought to be a town somewhere, seemed. Stretching, he moved to the front of the tree, and raising his hand to his brow, swept the country before him with a searching gaze.

A man slightly taller than average, with cool gray eyes and an easy manner, he straightened as his glance picked up a streamer of smoke to the southwest. A settlement, finally. He grinned at the discovery, relishing the thought of a good restaurant-cooked meal, a bed with springs and mattress. Seven days and nights under the sky were plenty; he'd gone longer stretches than that before without even thinking about it, but somehow he felt the need for the luxuries this time. He guessed maybe that year in the pen had turned him soft.

Lake grinned, considering the thought that a time behind bars could turn any man soft. The exact opposite was always true; a fellow came out tougher, harder, and filled with a certain grimness. It was natural, something that couldn't be avoided and likely would never leave him.

Wheeling, he moved back to the bay, stepped to the saddle. Roweling the big horse gently, he headed down the slope, pointing for the thin bands of smoke in the distance. He'd shake the taint of prison walls if folks would let him, he had several times assured himself. All he wanted was to build a new life, get a fresh start. It shouldn't be too difficult in a new country.

Two hours later he broke out of a screen of low foothills that lay around the foot of a towering pine-clad mountain and rode into a broad valley in which the town lay. San Sabal, a canted sign at a fork in the road a few miles back had said the place was called, and judging from the herds of cattle he had noted along the way, the valley was given mostly to raising beef. A fair-sized river cut the land near center—a resource that undoubtedly guaranteed year-around water for the spreads that lay along its banks.

The town itself, he saw as he turned into the end of its single and main street, was larger than he had first thought. Quite a number of stores lined the way, and back of them on either side were many residences. Idly, he noted the printed names on the false-fronted buildings, some freshly painted, all fairly new looking and well cared for. Yet the town was not a new one; the structures themselves proved that. It was simply that San Sabal was a progressive settlement, believed in keeping itself up and not permitting things to deteriorate as did most frontier towns.

The White Eagle Saloon. . . . The broad front of that establishment caught Lake Oliver's attention, and he angled the bay toward its hitchrack. A few doors down stood a taller two-storied structure: the Cattle Queen Hotel. That would work out fine. He'd have a drink or two and a meal in the White

Eagle, then put up for the night in its neighbor, the Cattle Queen.

Halting at the rack, he came off the saddle, again glad to have solid ground under his feet. Several persons were on the board sidewalks that bordered each side of the street, were moving slowly along, enjoying the coolness that was beginning to settle in with the end of day.

Directly opposite, Lake noted the office of the town marshal. A thin dark man of about his own age leaned against the door frame, eyed him narrowly. Deputy Marshal, the nickeled star on his shirt pocket confirmed. Oliver nodded to him coolly as he mounted the steps to the saloon's porch, crossed, and pushed through the swinging doors.

A lone bartender stood behind the long counter ranged against the opposite wall. In front and to its left was a scatter of tables and chairs. Only a handful of patrons was in evidence, and Lake could see no one in the adjacent room where faro and other gambling games were held. . . . A bit early yet for the evening trade, he guessed.

Pulling up to the bar, he nodded to the round-faced, balding man waiting for him to speak, and said, "Whiskey."

The bartender nodded, reached for a bottle and glass, poured a generous shot and slid it to him.

"On the house—first time," he said. "Custom of mine. Name's Tom McCoy. My place. Always pleasured to welcome a stranger."

Oliver grinned, downed the liquor. "Obliged to you. Right nice layout you've got here. Any chance a man could get a meal?"

"Sure thing," McCoy replied, filling Lake's glass again. "Got a regular kitchen in the back."

"Fine. Can use the works—whatever's the day's special."

"Steak and fried potatoes—that's the special every day. About all anybody around here eats. Set yourself at one of the tables and I'll holler at the cook."

McCoy moved off, and picking up his drink, Oliver crossed to a table near the end of the bar, settled contentedly onto a chair. It was pleasant in the shadowy room filled with the good odors of tobacco smoke, liquor, and a touch of perfume still remaining from last night's presence of saloon girls.

The big hanging lamps were not yet lit for the night and there was a softness to all things, a gentleness that would vanish later when the crowd started pouring in through the batwings and business as usual got under way.

Lake let his eyes halt on the three men near the center of the bar. All were up in their fifties, he guessed; one, a tall, well-built man, seemed better dressed than the others. Russ, one of his friends had called him. The man next to him looked to be a working rancher: lean, sharp, windburned face with deep-set eyes and graying hair. Third of the group was also thin and graying, but he sported a neat square-cut beard and thick mustache. He could be a merchant or—

Oliver's thoughts halted as the door beyond the bar opened and a young Mexican carrying a platter of food entered. Behind him, bearing cup and a small pot of coffee, was McCoy. Both crossed to his table, set the meal before him, and stepped back.

"You want anything else," the saloonman said, "just sing out."

Lake nodded, looked over the well-filled plate with longing, filled his nostrils with the smells of the tempting food.

11

"Looks like everything I'll be needing is right here," he said, and picked up his knife and fork.

McCoy murmured something and turned away, making a comment to the three at the bar. Savoring his first mouthful of the meal, Lake only vaguely heard his voice, but from the tail of his eye he saw the man straighten, come half around as the batwings swung in.

He shifted his attention to that point, saw the deputy he'd noticed on the street when he rode in. With him was a larger man wearing the marshal's badge. The lawman was redheaded, had a ruddy face and hard blue eyes.

Lake came up slowly as he saw the pair was headed for his table. Laying down his knife and fork, tension suddenly building within him, he placed his hands flat on the table and leaned back, looked up questioningly at the lawmen now halted before him.

The marshal, jaw set, glared at him belligerently. "Your name Oliver?"

Chapter TWO

Lake nodded coldly. "That's me. What's on your mind?"

The lawman hooked thumbs on his belt, thrust his head forward. "I'm Rufe Dillow, marshal of this town. I want to know what you're doing here."

"Passing through," Oliver drawled.

"That all?" Dillow demanded suspiciously. "You saying you ain't aiming to hang around?"

Oliver crossed his arms over his chest. "Come to think on it, was figuring to spend the night at the hotel. I've been straddling my horse for—"

"Climb back on him and keep going, mister!"

There was complete silence within the saloon. Outside in the street a rider was moving by, the soft thud of his horse's hooves in the dust falling in a methodic beat.

"Why?"

The question infuriated Rufe Dillow. "You know why, dammit! I got a clean town here, one where there ain't never no trouble. Done that by keeping outlaws and convicts like you out."

The tall, well-built man Lake had heard someone call Russ came a step away from the bar, his features intent.

"You mean he's escaped from somewhere, Rufe?"

The lawman shook his head. "Nope, never said that. Said he was a convict—"

"Not now," Lake cut in quietly. "Done my time. It's all back of me."

"Then you mean he's an ex-convict," Russ said. "Big difference."

"Not to me," Dillow snapped. "Once a man's served a stretch the poison's there. He'll always be an outlaw. Minute I seen him ride in—"

"Was me that seen him," the deputy said, frowning.

"Minute Jessup seen him, I figured trouble was here. He was in for robbing a stagecoach up Wyoming way. Spent a year in the pen for it. Just got out, near as I can figure from the dodger. . . . Probably scouting around right now for something easy to—"

"On my way to Arizona. Got a job waiting for me there." Oliver broke into the marshal's words again.

Temper was stirring within him. This was the third time he'd encountered the law since his release, and as before, the men wearing the badge had met him with hostility and unreasonableness. He guessed it would always be that way, at least until the passing of years enabled him to live it down.

Dillow bobbed his head, shrugged. "All right, I'm taking you at your word—but you'll do your sleeping somewheres else, not in my town."

Lake Oliver stared moodily at the lawman. Harsh words sprang to his lips, but he pressed them back. It was an argument he couldn't win regardless of right or wrong. A sardonic grin pulled down the corners of his mouth.

"It all right if I finish my eating, Marshal?"

Dillow eyed him narrowly. "Just be damned sure you're on your way soon's you're finished."

McCoy leaned back against his bar, clucked softly. "Don't hardly seem right, Rufe, your running a man off like this. He wants to stay the night, he ought—"

"Not in my town," Dillow said stubbornly. "That's the way things get started—letting a jasper like him hang around."

"Aims to ride on in the morning," Russ pointed out.

"What he says, anyway, but come sunup he'll find a reason to stay over till noon. Then first thing you know it'll be dark and too late for him to head out so it'll be another night. Hell, I know his kind. My business to know them."

"Reckon we oughtn't blame Rufe," the older rancher said, turning and taking up his drink. "We elected him to run a clean town. Best thing we can do is let him do it his own way."

The saloonman glanced up. "Maybe so, Ben, but a man's got rights, too. Free country. No law says he can't ride across the land, eat and sleep where he wants long as he don't bother nobody and's got the cash to pay up."

"Unless he's a convicted outlaw," Dillow declared in a loud voice. "Man's record proves he is, and the way to keep the kind of town you want is to run off the likes of him quick as they show up."

Oliver, listening patiently to it all while continuing to eat, raised his glance.

"You can quit your worrying, Marshal. Meant I'd move on soon as I'm finished. You don't want me around, I sure won't stay."

Rufe Dillow seemed momentarily startled by the

15

bland announcement. He looked around the room, settled his attention on his deputy.

"I'm leaving it to you, Cal. See that he does. I got some business that's needing looking after."

Jessup shifted his shoulders, waited until the marshal had turned and left the building. Then, with a nod at Oliver, said: "I'll be watching from across the street. You ain't out of here and on your way in thirty minutes, I'm coming after you. Hear?"

Lake bobbed his head. "Whatever you say, Deputy," he replied, and watched the lawman wheel and shoulder his way through the swinging doors.

Anger still simmering within him, Oliver resumed his meal. He was reaching the point where he was accustomed to such treatment, but he knew he could never accept it without becoming riled. He was expected to pay for his mistake forever, it would seem, and most everyone, particularly lawmen, were determined not to let him forget he had once been convicted of a crime and served a term in prison for it.

But then each time, after the deep-set anger cooled and he thought about it, he saw it all in a different light. Lawmen should be suspicious, he supposed. And a man with a record—a holdup record especially—was one they would naturally be most leery of.

"It's a damned shame—"

At Tom McCoy's words Oliver paused, lifted his gaze. The saloonman was staring through the doorway into the street beyond. Cal Jessup had taken up a position in front of the marshal's office and was waiting.

Lake stirred indifferently. "Starting to get used to it. Reason why I'm heading for Arizona. Figure things'll be different."

"Lawmen there, too."

"But Arizona's a far piece from Wyoming, and maybe the badge toters out that way won't be hunting trouble like this marshal of yours."

McCoy brushed impatiently at his receding hair. "That Rufe! Election's coming this fall and he figure's he's got to do a lot of loud-mouthing around. Always out to make hisself a mark so's folks'll know what a good marshal he is."

"They're all pretty much alike," Oliver said, pouring himself a final cup of coffee. "Most of them are proud and like their jobs."

"Maybe so, but I'm sure getting a gutful of Rufe. So's everybody else, I think. Good chance he won't get hisself reelected. There's a good man running against him this time—something that ain't ever happened before."

"Oh?"

McCoy half turned, thumbed at the three men standing before the bar. "Fellow there in the brown suit—name of Russ Sadilek. He's bucking for the job, too."

Lake shrugged. "Shows you how wrong a man can be. I had him figured for a big-time rancher."

"Was that—once. Fine place north of here. Sold out a couple years ago to some English bunch—a syndicate. Been sort of taking it easy ever since. Been said he's running short on money and that's why he's wanting the badge, but I got my doubts about that."

"Fine-looking man," Lake commented, "but it takes more'n that to be a marshal, or any kind of a lawman. The hard-nosed ones folks don't cotton to generally make the best ones. . . . Sure not a job for a man if he's out to make friends."

"Reckon not, but there's times when they go too

17

far. Merchants of a town got to make a living, too, and running off customers, high-handed like—"

"Can chalk that up to the cost of having a clean town," Lake said dryly. "It's all right. I don't mind. Got to where I sort've expect it. . . . Was a fine meal."

McCoy smiled. "You get enough?"

"Was a plenty. What's the damages?"

"Oh, a dollar'll cover everything—whiskey and all."

Lake Oliver pushed back his chair and rose to his feet. Digging into a pocket, he produced the necessary coin.

"Obliged to you for speaking up for me. Man with a convict tag around his neck is always a mite short of friends, especially in a strange town."

McCoy's shoulders stirred. "Don't think it's right for him to have to keep on paying for something when he's settled up once, that's all. Be like me following you down the street wanting to collect another dollar from you for your grub."

"Won't argue with you there, but I'm learning that's the way it goes," Oliver said, reaching for his sack of tobacco and fold of papers. Taking one of the small, thin sheets, he began to roll a cigarette.

The saloonman studied him thoughtfully, taking note of the low-slung pistol with its worn grips, the careless yet coiled ease of the man.

"You really aiming to ride on or was you just ridding yourself of Rufe?"

"Riding on. Not looking for trouble. Not worth it for something that don't amount to anything."

McCoy said, "Well, don't blame you, much as I'd like to see somebody tell Rufe to go to hell. Can see why you wouldn't. Man has to sort of walk careful once he's spent time behind bars."

18

Lake was silent, allowed a thin stream of smoke to curl up from his nostrils and twist into the stilled air of the saloon.

"For a fact," he said finally. "Reckon I'd best not keep that deputy waiting. . . . So long. Obliged to you again."

McCoy bobbed his head. "You ever back this way, drop in. Always be welcome—and maybe by then we'll have us a lawman with a little sense. . . . Now, if you're wanting a good place to camp, ride down along the river. Folks do a lot of picnicking there. You'll find a bunch of nice spots."

Oliver smiled his thanks, touched the men lounging at the bar with his glance, and started for the swinging doors. Pushing his way through, he crossed the porch and stepped down to the hitchrack where the bay waited. Without bothering to look at the scowling Cal Jessup, he mounted and rode off down the street.

He'd enjoyed a fine meal, guessed he could wait another day or two for that bed with springs and a mattress.

Chapter THREE

Five miles or so below the settlement, Lake Oliver drew the bay to a halt. As McCoy had said, there were many good camping places along the river, and he chose one where a gouge in the face of a low bluff formed an alcove and made for natural shelter from the wind that lifted each morning with sunrise to sweep the land.

He was tired from the long day, and after seeing to the gelding's needs, stripped off his clothing, took a quick dip in the cold water of the stream, and then, rolling up in his blanket and tarp, went to sleep.

He was awake at first light and up and about while the still-hidden sun was tinging a scatter of fragment d clouds hanging above the horizon to a vivid salmon. By the time the glowing disk had pushed its rim over the line of rugged hills in the east, he had eaten his breakfast of fried pork, hardtack and coffee, was packed and ready to ride on.

He had thought little about the incident in San Sabal, having now, after previous similar occasions, something of an understanding of the minds of lawmen. He reckoned he could not blame them, supposed that if he were a man wearing a star and responsible for the well-being of a town insofar as law and order was concerned, he'd likely be just as wary of known outlaws—prison terms behind them or not.

But it was nevertheless getting a bit trying, and he could only wish that all the well-circulated wanted dodgers that had been issued on him and that yet remained in the offices of marshals and sheriffs across the western frontier could somehow be destroyed and forgotten. Then, perhaps, he could move about in peace.

Taking a final glance around his camp to see that he had overlooked nothing, he swung onto the bay and settled himself on the saddle. It was going to be another hot day; he could tell by the emptiness of the sky, already changing to an arch of transparent steel. Hopefully, by dark he would have reached another town—one that would not begrudge him a night's comfortable lodging.

Lifting the reins he wheeled the bay about, pointed him south along the river. He'd follow the stream as long as it didn't change course; it would be cooler—

The sudden hollow crack of a rifle and a spurt of dust a few yards ahead of the gelding brought him up short. Hand dropping to the pistol at his hip, he pivoted the bay, threw his glance back up to the crown of the gentle slope to his left.

A half a dozen riders, ranged in a line, guns leveled, were looking down on him. Slightly to their fore was Marshal Rufe Dillow. A bit to his right was the deputy, Cal Jessup. The others he did not know.

"Get your hands up!"

Dillow's command reached him. Wondering, cursing softly, Lake Oliver raised his arms. At once the riders moved off the rim, came to him, spreading into a half circle before him.

"What the hell's this all about?" Lake demanded roughly as temper flared through him. He was abruptly fed up with Dillow and his overzealous devotion to the law.

The marshal's eyes blazed. "You got the guts of an army mule—asking that!" he snarled.

"Maybe—but I still want to know what this means. I rode out of your town like I said I would, headed for Arizona—"

"You ain't headed there now," Jessup said, and laughed. "Only place you're going is to a hanging."

"Hanging?"

"What he said," Dillow replied. "Knew when you showed up there was something stewing. If I'd a had any sense I'd've locked you up yesterday. . . . Old man Hilton'd be alive then."

"Hilton? Who's Hilton?" Oliver asked coldly. "What's he got to do with me?"

"Better to say what did you do to him. Killed him, that's what, when you robbed his bank."

Lake swore in disgust. "You're loco, Marshal. Been right here since late yesterday afternoon. Never left my camp from the time I got here."

"Sure, sure. Expected you'd say that. What you ain't saying is that you and your gang of hard-cases—"

"Gang—that's crazy, too! I'm by myself. Look around—you won't find any tracks but my own. . . . Marshal, what're you trying to do, pin something on me just because I once got myself in trouble and went to jail for it?"

"Got nothing to do with it—except it sort of maybe proves to me and everybody else that you're the kind that would do it. But we don't need that thinking. You was seen riding out after it was all over."

Lake Oliver drew himself up stiffly. "Whoever said this is a damned liar."

"Was a man on a white-stockinged bay—and built the same as—"

Oliver groaned in disgust. "For hell sake, Marshal, there's dozens of bay horses around—more of them than any other color, I expect. You can't go by that."

"Witness said it looked like you on the saddle."

"Looked like—that's no proof, either. Whoever your witness is had better do some thinking about it. Sure wasn't me."

The rider next to Jessup leaned forward, unhooked his rope, began to shape a loop. "Can't see as there's much sense waiting, Marshal. We know what the committee—"

Dillow swept the man with a hard look. "Put that rope away, Hazen. Thing's going to be done right—legal. Be up to them to decide and give the word."

"What's the use of waiting? You know same as the rest of us there ain't no doubt."

"He's right, Rufe," another of the posse added. "Him and them three that was with him was spotted when they rode off from the bank. Was you yourself found old man Hilton laying there on the floor dead, his head caved in and the safe empty. What else you need?"

"I don't need nothing," the lawman replied blandly. "But he's still got to stand up before the committee. My job to see he does that. They do the deciding."

Oliver, listening in silence as a mixture of anger and alarm built within him, considered Dillow's florid face.

23

"What's this committee you keep talking about?"

"Law committee," the marshal said. "Runs the town. We come up against something like what you've done and they figure what the punishment will be—"

"Hangmen!" Oliver said harshly. "What about a judge and a jury? Don't you believe in—"

"Judge!" one of the riders echoed. "Hell, we ain't seen one of them in over a year!"

Dillow nodded. "Henry's right. Judge's got such a big territory to cover he don't get here very often. Make no difference, anyway. He'd approve the sentence the committee will hand out. Always has."

"Which'll be a hanging," Henry said.

Lake shifted helplessly. Dillow and his men were convinced he had been in on the robbery and killing, probably assumed him to be the leader of the outlaw gang since he was a known ex-convict. Such would automatically elevate him to that position. And, far-fetched as it all was, he was in a tight spot.

He had to come up with something—proof of some sort they would listen to, but in the face of claims made by so-called witnesses, that would be hard to do. A man camping alone, having no visitors and seeing no passersby, was trapped between a rock and a high wall when it came to proving his whereabouts—especially to men who had already made up their minds.

Stall—hold them off as long as possible and maybe something would turn up—something that would help; that was all Lake Oliver could think to do.

"When'd this robbery and killing that I'm supposed to have done happened?" he asked, shrugging wearily.

"You know when," Dillow snapped. "Don't get cute with me."

"Not trying to. Just like to know when it was."

"Sometime after midnight. Hilton was working on his books, I figure. Seeing him in there must've fit right in with your scheming."

"My scheming?"

Dillow swore angrily, spat. "You going to say now you didn't ride into town yesterday with a plan all worked out to bust into the bank, grab off all the money there?"

"Just what I'm telling you—on my oath or word or anything you want. I had nothing to do with it—"

"That's sure a crock of bull," one of the riders cut in sharply. "We know better."

"You don't know anything," Oliver shot back. "You're guessing—and you're trying to make me the goat."

"Know what I seen," Cal Jessup declared. "You and them three others a riding away from behind the bank, splitting up and heading out into all different directions."

Lake studied the deputy closely. "You the witness the marshal's talking about?"

"He's one of them," Dillow said, answering for his man. "Couple others, too. . . . Let's cut out this jawing and get back to town. Could be them other posses have nabbed the rest of his bunch by now."

"Don't figure they'd go far," Henry said, nodding. "Not with him still here. . . . Expect we'll find the money in his saddlebags."

Lake Oliver, seeing a glimmer of hope in that, smiled grimly. "You're welcome to look through everything I've got—"

"Forget it," Dillow said. "He wouldn't be fool enough to do that—not after tipping his hand

25

yesterday by showing hisself in town. He knowed we'd go looking for him first off and he sure wouldn't want the money on him. It'll be with one of the others, or maybe cached somewheres."

Henry settled back. "Expect you're right, Marshal. Sure was lucky you spotted him—"

"Was me that done the spotting," Jessup said, again bringing the fact to the attention of others. "I remembered him from that dodger we got."

"Yeh, was lucky," Dillow said. "Reckon I'd've noticed him anyhow before the day was over—when I was making the rounds. Makes no difference. We seen him come in and now we got him. Next thing's to lock him up and run down the rest of the bunch."

"Could be they're figuring to meet up somewhere close to here, Rufe," Hazen said. "You think of that? They sure got to get together and split up all that money sometime. And their kind ain't much for trusting each other. They'll aim to do it right away."

Dillow frowned, scrubbed at his jaw. "Hell, yes, I thought of that. But there'd be no sense in us just setting around here looking and waiting. I aim to sweat this jasper a mite once I get him locked inside a cell, make him say where and when the meeting's to be."

"Save time was we to work him over right here. Could throw a rope around him—"

"Now, goddammit—there'll be no lynching—"

"Not figuring to, just want to do a little dragging around. We start scraping off some of his hide and I'm betting he'll speak right up, tell us where he's meeting his *compadres*."

"Just might work at that," Dillow said thoughtfully. "And with him being holed up here, could

26

mean they're planning to get together some place close."

"What I'm saying! Could save a powerful lot of time."

Lake Oliver, eyes narrowed, waited tensely. The odds were all wrong, but he wasn't about to let himself be dragged around over the flats in an effort to force him to talk, confess something he knew nothing about.

"All right, go ahead. Let's give him a dose—"

At Dillow's words Lake reacted instantly. He dropped his arms, threw himself forward on the saddle, and jammed spurs into the bay's flanks.

The big gelding, still far from completely broken, lunged ahead. He collided solidly with the smaller sorrel being ridden by the man uncoiling his rope. Rider and horse slammed back against those behind him, sent them all shying off, struggling to stay upright.

Dillow shouted an oath, swung up his pistol. Lake struck out at him with a balled fist, but the bay was plunging away erratically for the brush beyond the riders and the blow missed its mark. It caught the lawman on the chest, served only to deter him briefly, destroy his aim.

Drawing his own weapon as the gelding legged it for the dense undergrowth, Lake Oliver started to twist about, lay a warning shot at the milling horses and cursing men. In that same fragment of time Rufe Dillow fired again. Lake felt a searing stab of pain in his leg—knew he'd been hit—hit bad.

Chapter *FOUR*

Oliver cut the bay sharp right when he rounded the squat butte, and rode hard for a stand of head-high willows and nodding sunflowers. Pain was roaring through him, and his left leg from thigh down seemed wet and warm, and his boot appeared to be filling with blood.

More gunshots flatted through the morning stillness, and just beyond him he heard the vicious clipping sound of bullets slicing through leaves.

"Get after him—goddammit!"

Rufe Dillow's voice was a wild bellow that echoed along the trees. An answer was shouted back, but the words were lost to Lake as guns opened up once again and more bullets peppered the brush through which he had just passed.

They were all behind him, unseen, but the racket of their horses and weapons was guide enough. He veered sharp again at the lower end of the bluff, suddenly found himself again in the clearing near the hollow where he had spent the night. He hauled up short, aware that the sounds of pursuit were fading, that the lawman and his posse had thought he had continued, were driving straight through the brush for the grove of trees beyond.

He sucked in a deep breath, looked down at the wound in his leg. The bullet had entered the fleshy part halfway between hip and knee. The slug had missed bone but torn a long gash that was bleeding heavily. One thing was certain: he had to stop the flow or he'd be a dead man in mighty quick time. He was already beginning to feel light-headed.

Listening briefly for sounds of the riders and deciding that they were still moving away, he dug into his saddlebags, procured an old undershirt. He tried to rip it down center, failed. Impatiently, he drew his skinning knife and slashed the cloth into a wide strip.

Folding the length several times to form a band, he applied it directly to the wound, pulled it tight, wincing at the pain. Jaw set, he cinched the cloth with a knot. He sat motionless then, staring at the makeshift bandage in a dazed sort of way.

The cloth reddened slowly, but he had checked the severe bleeding. It would work for a while, but Oliver knew he'd have to have proper medical attention for such a bad gunshot wound soon. There'd be a doctor back in San Sabal, but going there was out of the question; as well let himself bleed to death as return and put his neck in the noose that awaited him. Both meant the end for him.

He roused, looked off across the river. There could be another town not too far—or a ranch. That would be his best bet, a ranch—Abruptly his thoughts came to a stop as his flagging senses, alerted by sheer instinct, caught the thud of approaching horses. The posse had discovered its mistake, was backtracking.

Oliver glanced about desperately. Brush along the bank of the river grew thick, nourished by an ever-present store of water. He was too much in the open where he was—in the hollow of the butte—and besides, it would be easy to get cornered. His best chances lay near the stream.

Urging the bay forward, he rode down to the edge of the water. The horse balked, unwilling to breast the flowing, muddy current. Oliver roweled him impatiently, forced him on. The gelding lunged into the water, caught his balance, and began to wade. Once again using spurs, Lake brought him in close to the overhanging growth and halted, praying the gelding wouldn't be turned restless by the water purling about his legs and set up a disturbance.

The moments dragged, became minutes. Tension mounted within Lake, kept pace with the steady, stabbing throb in his thigh. He stiffened then as the muffled thud of a horse almost upon him reached his ears.

"See any sign of him over there?"

It was Cal Jessup's voice. The deputy had guessed he'd doubled back to the gouge in the butte—but his hunch had come a couple of minutes too late.

"Nope. Still figure he made a run for the hills."

The reply came from somewhere in the brush to the left of the bluff.

"You look in that coulee?"

"Sure did. Ain't there."

Jessup swore. "Was sure he'd try fooling us, drop back to where we jumped him first. Guess I was wrong."

"Yeh. . . . One thing sure, he ain't going far—not with that bullet in him. Where's the marshal?"

"Working the grove. Reckon we might as well catch up—but keep your eyes peeled."

The bay shifted, swished his tail at the horde of gnats swarming about him. Oliver's pulse quickened

30

and his hand moved to the pistol on his hip. He didn't want to shoot; he had no real quarrel with Jessup or any of the men in the posse, but he wasn't going to be taken and railroaded onto a scaffold for hanging.

"You coming?"

It was the man near the butte. A moment later the quiet *tunk-a-tunk* of Jessup's horse moving off came to Lake.

"I'm coming. . . . Thought I heard something. Was nothing, I guess. Maybe a rabbit scooting off through the brush."

Oliver breathed deeper. He waited out several long minutes and then cut the bay back around to the sloping edge where he'd ridden him into the water. Halting there, the horse still in the river, he leaned far over and peered around the dense-growing willows. Cal Jessup and the man with him were gone.

He eased back in the saddle, favored the injured leg by resting as little weight on it as possible. It was difficult to do; by the very act of sitting the hull he was forcing pressure upon the wound, causing it to continue bleeding. But it would be a mistake to dismount. He'd never muster enough strength to walk—and climbing back onto the bay would be out of the question. Help was what he needed; he had to find help.

He spurred the gelding out of the stream, headed him north into the direction opposite of that taken by Rufe Dillow and the posse. There were other riders out in search of him, too, he must remember that. Several groups, according to what the lawman had said.

It couldn't be avoided. He'd have to take his chances, and logic assured him they were best in an area away from where he had first been encountered. If luck was with him he'd slip by the others.

The bay moved on, walking at a quick, eager pace, following the path that bordered the bank of the river. Lake was feeling greater pain, the wound being aggravated by the constant motion of the horse, but there was no way around that; he'd just have to bear it. Reaching up, he brushed at the sweat clothing his brow, his face, misting his eyes, and strained to see ahead. There were buildings of some sort in the distance—he thought. He could not be sure. Everything was clouded, hazy, was continually fading in and out of his vision. He reckoned he could be imagining things, too.

Maybe he was riding back into town.

That thought drove into his consciousness, caused him to pull the gelding to a stop. He leaned forward, shaded his eyes unsteadily, tried to make out the vague blurs. It wasn't the town; he was sure of that. There weren't enough buildings—only four or five. . . . Somebody's ranch. There was a sign. *B. Carr,* he thought it read.

Wearily he sank back into the saddle, grabbed for the horn to save himself from falling. Unbidden, the bay resumed his stride.

A sharp sound, like the crack of a door banging shut, brought Lake out of his lethargy. He opened his eyes, struggled to focus them. The gelding had halted, was standing before a hitchrack in a clean-swept yard. Beyond the poles stood a long, low-roofed house with a gallery running its width. Two dim, indefinite shapes were hurrying toward him. A man and a girl.

"Shot—" he managed to say, forcing a tight grin. "Be obliged to you if—"

Lake's words trailed off into nothing as the man

32

came into sharper focus, stopped. A thin, gray-haired individual with a sharp, disapproving, angry face. Oliver remembered. He'd been one of the three men standing at the bar of the White Eagle. Ben, someone had called him. That, plus the name on the sign—he'd be Ben Carr.

"What the hell you want?"

The rancher's tone was harsh, hostile. Lake shifted his gaze to the girl. She was young, pretty, and there was a frown on her features.

"Need help—some patching up. Appreciate it if—"

"Keep riding!" Carr snapped. "Don't want you around here. Not about to get mixed up with no outlaw."

"Not—an outlaw," Oliver said doggedly. "I—"

"The hell you ain't! I was in the saloon yesterday, heard what Rufe Dillow said. What's more, you owned up to it."

"Owned up to being who I am. Served my time for—"

"Papa—he needs help," the girl broke in. "He's hurt—been shot, looks like."

The rancher whirled upon her. "Stay out of this, Julie! Only cause trouble, was we to lend him a hand. Let him go somewheres else."

"Somewhere else? Where would that be?"

"No business of ours where it is—hear? We plain ain't mixing in his trouble. Don't know what he's gone and done, but it won't be nothing good. You help him it'll be the same as being in it with him."

"You don't know, Papa. It could have been some kind of an accident."

Ben Carr was silent for a brief moment. Then, having given the girl's thought the consideration due it, looked closely at Lake.

33

"Who shot you, mister?"

The rancher's voice seemed far off, was barely audible through the dense fog that surrounded Lake Oliver. He shook his head to clear it.

"The marshal—Dillow. Was trying to—"

"You see!" Carr yelled the words at Julie. "You see what you'd be letting us in for? He's done something bad, maybe killed somebody in town. Rufe set out after him, put a bullet in his leg."

Abruptly the rancher took a step toward Oliver. "Get out of here—you understand? You hear me? Don't want you on my place! Don't even want nobody seeing you around! Go on, get cracking!"

The words registered dully on Lake Oliver's mind, their meaning finally working through to him. Drawing stiffly upright on the saddle, he steadied himself with one hand on the horn, lifted the reins with the other.

"Obliged—just the same," he mumbled, and cut the gelding about for the gate.

In the next instant a wave of darkness engulfed him. A great swirling rushed through his head, and he knew he was falling.

Chapter *FIVE*

Lake could hear a meadowlark. The clear, sweet whistling of the bird came to him through an open window near the bed upon which he lay.

His eyes remained fixed on the faintly stirring lace curtains that covered the opening while a curious detachment and lack of interest in all things filled him. Once before he had experienced such apathy—a time when he had taken a bullet in his chest and also lost a vast amount of blood. It was pure weakness, he knew—and didn't care.

His thoughts organized slowly, tiredly, and it was some time before it all came to him. The bay had carried him into the yard of Ben Carr's ranch. He had asked for aid from the rancher and a girl named Julie—the man's daughter, he supposed. He'd been refused, ordered off the premises. He had turned to go—and that was the end of it. He had blacked out.

Now he was inside a house, on a clean, soft bed in a light, airy room—Julie's, he reckoned, judging from the furnishings, and assuming it was the Carr house. If so, the rancher would be in a state over it, being forced to take him in, probably at the girl's insistence. Carr was a tough old man, he could see that—even with Julie, whom he seemed to dominate with a harsh hand. It was a wonder the rancher had permitted her to help at all.

Looking down he saw that, except for his boots, he was still fully dressed. There was a tightness about his leg indicating the presence of a bandage. Ben Carr would have been forced to help Julie with that little chore, he thought, and grinned wryly at the realization.

He'd best be up and on his way. Carr was right about one thing: his presence there could only mean trouble for them.

Head now clear, he put his hand palm down on the covers, tried to raise himself. The effort sent a wave of nausea surging through him, and half upright, he hung for a moment and then gave it up, lay back. He was worse off for strength than he'd figured.

He became aware then of a figure standing in the doorway. It was Julie. She had watched him make his try and now, disapproval on her smooth features, came on into the room.

"Best you forget that," she said, halting beside the bed. "You're not going anywhere—not for a while, anyway."

He frowned, shook his head. "Can't stay here. Means trouble for you and your pa. Dillow and his posse—"

"Oh, fiddle-faddle to Rufe Dillow!" she said with an impatient wave of her hands. "He won't dare come into this house."

"Your pa—he'll probably tell him—"

"Probably. But he's gone and won't be back until dark, and by then, maybe—"

"No maybe to it. I'll have to be out of here by then." Lake paused, remembering. "My horse—he

36

shouldn't be out where he can be spotted. Somebody'll see him, know I'm holed up in here. He's the big thing they're going on."

"I put him in the barn. What do you mean—the big thing they're going on?"

"One of the bunch that robbed the bank and killed some man named Hilton last night rode off on a bay like mine. Dillow and everyone else around's got it in their head that it was me."

The girl was studying him intently. "Is that why you were shot?"

Oliver realized then that she knew nothing of the incident that had occurred. Word of it had not yet reached the ranch. He nodded, told her of what had happened as it was related to him by Rufe Dillow.

"Figured I'd not stand a chance with them already convicting me and just sweating to put a rope around my neck—so I made a run for it. That's when I got shot. Was looking for help when my horse wandered into your yard."

"Good thing he did," Julie said primly. "Another hour or two and you would have bled to death."

"Know that, and I'm obliged to you and your pa—"

"Not him," the girl said quietly. "He was for putting you back on your horse and driving him off. I—I managed to talk him out of it."

She looked toward the window, her eyes going to the long flat and distant hills beyond. "Was the first time I ever stood up to him," she murmured.

Lake Oliver reached for her hand, pressed it gently. "Mighty sorry I've caused trouble between you and him. Sure didn't aim to."

"I'm glad you did. I never had the courage to oppose him before." Julie paused, listened. The lark was still pouring his song into the morning air. "Pa is sort of hard to get along with," she continued finally. "He's been that way ever since my mother died—ten years ago. I don't think he actually wants to be mean—I think it's because he's so terribly lonely."

"Probably is," Oliver said, feeling a drowsiness crawling up into him. It was becoming an effort to carry on the conversation—something he was enjoying and hoped would not end. "I guess I owe you plenty for the doctoring job. Don't see how you managed it alone."

"Wasn't me alone. Our cook, Crucita, helped me. She's Mexican—and a wonder with medicine. Makes them up from herbs and plants and such."

"Expect that hole in my leg was pretty bad."

Julie nodded. "The bullet went clear through, though. I found it in your boot when I took it off. It had hit the leather of your saddle or something, and dropped. The good thing about it was that it missed the bone."

"Reckon I was lucky there. . . . Still got a feeling I ought to get out of here."

"Maybe by dark. You're too weak now, after losing so much blood. Doubt if you can stand, much less sit a saddle and ride. But you're coming out of it. I've been feeding you once every hour."

"Feeding me?"

Julie smiled. "Yes, a broth Crucita cooked up. I've been sort of pouring it down you ever since we finished doctoring your leg."

Lake stirred. "Sure don't recollect—"

"You were out. Crucita had to hold you while I spooned the broth. It's the only reason you've got strength enough now to talk."

Oliver shook his head in bewilderment. He had been unaware of any of it.

38

"If we keep on with the broth, you ought to be able to travel by night. Your leg won't be well, of course, but you'll have your strength back."

"Must be strong stuff—"

"It is. I don't know what all she puts in it, chicken for one thing, and whiskey. Know that. Then there's some kind of herb she gets down by the river."

He shifted again restlessly, nervously. He was becoming more and more concerned by his presence in the Carr house. If Dillow, or any of the posses, found him there it would go hard for the girl and her father—aiding and hiding a wanted killer, that's what they'd say. And it would be doubly tough on Julie since she was doing it all against Ben Carr's wishes.

"Still think this is the wrong place for me to be. How about the barn? There a place in it where I could wait until dark?"

Julie's lips tightened. "You'll stay right where you are," she declared firmly, and turned to the doorway. A squat, dark woman, smiling broadly and carrying a bowl and spoon, entered. She surveyed Lake critically.

"He is better, no?"

"Much better, Crucita," the girl replied, taking the broth from her. "He wants to leave."

"No—no," the older woman said, wagging her head. "Such would not be wise. With night, perhaps."

Oliver struggled to sit up, managed it partly this time. "Not perhaps, *señora,* for sure."

Crucita folded her arms across her ample bosom, considered him speculatively. "He is a stubborn one, eh?"

39

"Stubborn, but he'll do what I say," the girl replied, and began to feed Oliver from the bowl.

The broth was thick, had a sharp, bitter taste to it. Lake recoiled from his first mouthful, muttered: "Don't see how I failed to wake up when you started putting this into me."

"Swallow it," Julie said firmly, "and figure on more all the rest of the day. You're anxious to leave; all right, this is the only thing that will fix it so that you can."

Crucita bobbed her confirmation, watched for a time longer, and then turned and left the room. Julie completed the contents of the bowl, set it aside.

"That'll do for a while—a couple of hours, at least. It's more than I've been able to get down you all morning."

Lake grinned. "Can see why. Even a dead man would fight off that stuff. . . . But I'll swallow all you bring," he added hastily as Julie frowned, "if it'll put me back on my horse again."

"It will. I've seen it work before. Now, the best thing for you is sleep."

Lake glanced around the room. "My gun—"

The girl nodded. Turning, she took up his belt and holster with the smooth-handled forty-five thrust into it, passed it to him. He laid it alongside on the bed, within easy reach.

"Makes sleeping easier," he said, spacing the words slowly. There was something in the broth that made his eyes heavy, dulled his senses. He reckoned that was part of Crucita's treatment—sleep and—

Chapter *SIX*

The hammer of running horses, veering into the yard and halting, woke Lake Oliver.

He sat up instantly, momentarily surprised at his ability to do so, regretting also the sudden motion that sent a stab of pain through his leg. He had slept the entire day, being roused hourly and then only partially by Julie while she administered doses of Crucita's strength-restoring broth.

He felt much improved, fully recovered in fact except for the pain and stiffness in his leg, and pivoting, he dropped his feet over the edge of the bed and stood upright.

The stabbing in his thigh increased instantly, but he ignored it, glanced around for his boots while a strong urgency built within him. He located his footgear under the chair, sat down in it to pull them on.

"Ben! Ben Carr!"

The yell echoed through the silent house. Hurriedly stamping into his boots, Lake reached for his belt, strapped it about his waist. Pausing briefly to check the forty-five, he crossed to the front window of the room, peered out.

It was one of the posses—five men in all. They

41

had pulled up to the corner of the structure. He could see the rancher, with Julie at his side, moving up from the rear of the place. Evidently they had been engaged in some chore. Together, they faced the men.

A man wearing a red-and-black-checked shirt touched the brim of his hat to the girl, said, "You seen any strangers going by today?"

Carr's shoulders came back. "Reckon we have," he said cautiously. "Why?"

"Looking for a jailbird name of Lake Oliver. Got two killings chalked up against him."

Lake stiffened. Two killings?

"Name of God!" the rancher said. "Who?"

The rider leaned forward, brushed his hat to the back of his head. "Ain't you heard nothing about what's been happening in town?"

"Got my work to do. Been out on the range all day."

"Well, this here Oliver and three other hardcases robbed the bank last night. Killed old man Hilton doing it. Then this morning the marshal and some of the boys jumped Oliver down near the river. Shot it out with him. Rufe winged him but he gave them the slip, got away. Was a couple hours later Rufe come across him again. Marshal's dead."

Ben Carr stared at the man. "Dillow—you mean this Oliver killed him, too?"

"Way it looks."

Lake hung motionless and silent beside the window, scarcely breathing as the rider's words registered on his mind. . . . Two murders charged to him—and he had committed none. . . . What the hell was happening to him?

"Are you sure it was this—this Lake Oliver who did it?" Julie Carr's voice trembled slightly.

"Yes'm—well, fairly sure. Know for a fact he was in on the bank robbing and killing. And there can't be much doubt he's the one that shot down the marshal. Took place right close to where they jumped him the first time."

"But nobody saw it—"

"Well, no, reckon not exactly. The posse'd split up, was beating the brush down there along the river. They heard a shot, and all cut and run to where it come from. The deputy got to Rufe first but he was already dead and this here Oliver'd got away."

"But nobody knows for certain that Lake Oliver did it," Julie persisted.

The rider looked more closely at the girl. "Was him sure enough," he said doggedly.

"Had to be," Ben Carr broke in, tossing an angry glance at Julie. "And I can tell you where you can find him!"

The man in the checked shirt came up sharply, a surprised look on his swarthy face. "You can?"

"Yeh—right there inside my house. He's laying in there on a bed, shot in the leg."

There was a long moment of stunned silence. The posse leader finally found his voice. "But—how—"

"Rode in this morning, most dead from that bullet you said Rufe had put in him."

"And you took him in?"

"Wasn't aiming to. Figured he was mixed up in something. I was in McCoy's yesterday when Dillow ordered him out of the town. Anyway, he showed up here asking for help. Told him hell no and to keep on riding. He started to, but he was so far gone he plain fell off his horse.

"Girl of mine insisted on looking after him, fixing him up."

One of the riders laughed. "That's a plumb big favor to us and the committee. He'll be able to walk to his own hanging now."

The man in the checked shirt continued to stare at Carr. "How's it happen you didn't let nobody know about him being here? He some kind of friend of yourn?"

"Friend—hell, no! Never saw him before yesterday. And reason I didn't go hightailing it into town was that I didn't know what'd happened. Don't reckon I would have even if I had. Been a policy of mine to keep my nose out of other folks' business—"

"Killings around here are your business, Ben, same as they're everybody decent in the valley."

"Don't you go lecturing me, Deke!" the rancher snapped, suddenly aroused. "What I do's my business—and one thing I sure ain't got is time to get myself all mixed up in things that don't pertain to me. Short of help like I am I got more work than a man ought to have to do."

Deke shrugged, glanced over his shoulder to the men behind him, nodded, and swung down. The others followed, one of the party taking up all the reins and leading the horses to the nearby hitchrack.

"He still armed?"

"Reckon he is," Carr said. "Was wearing a gun when he showed up. He'll still have it."

Deke ran a nervous finger inside the collar of his heavy shirt, brushed at the sweat on his face. He drew his pistol, checked its loads. "Expect we'd best go at this careful like. He ain't going to come peaceable."

Julie started to turn for the house. Ben Carr caught at her hand, drew her back.

44

Deke touched the members of his posse with a look. "You all set?"

Lake Oliver delayed no further. Wheeling, wincing at the pain that shot through his leg, he recrossed the room to the window in the adjacent side wall, peered out. It let into a yard. Raising the sash, he stepped through.

Pausing there to locate the barn, he crouched low, made his way quickly alongside the house until he reached the hardpack at the rear of the structure. The barn was a long fifty or more strides on the far side. He stood a good chance of being seen as he moved into the open; he realized that— realized, too, that it was a risk he was compelled to take. Grim, still crouched low, and ignoring the throbbing in his stiffening leg, he continued on for the larger bulk of the barn.

He made it without incident, and breathless, he paused at its corner to rest. Turning, he threw a glance to the house. The posse, weapons drawn, were fanning out, preparing to surround the place. Julie and Ben Carr had drawn off to one side. The rancher's fingers were still locked about the girl's wrist, as if he feared she might yet break free and voice a warning to the man all assumed was inside the structure.

As Lake watched Carr swung about and faced the girl, began to speak rapidly, angrily. He probably was giving Julie a good dressing down for caring for him, Oliver thought, and wished there was some way he could thank the girl. He'd like to tell her that her faith in him was justified, too, that he was no killer but only a victim of circumstances. She didn't appear to believe the man they called Deke and the charges he voiced and he hoped she would

45

continue to feel that way; but with her father and all the others insisting she could change.

The doors to the barn lay at the opposite end of the wall that faced the yard. Endeavoring to enter from that opening would immediately expose him to the posse, now moving into position around the house. Pivoting slowly in deference to his wound, Oliver walked along the side until he reached the rear of the building. Two corrals lay off that end, and circling, he entered a sort of alley that led up to the back doors.

He stepped into the shadowy interior of the structure, hoping he'd not encounter any of the hired help, and drew to a stop in the center of the runway off which the stalls were built.

He located the bay in the end compartment. The gelding's gear had not been removed, probably at Ben Carr's insistence since he was supposed to be gone by sundown. Backing the animal into the cleared area, Oliver checked the cinch, taking no chances. It was still tight.

Once again he looked to the house. The posse riders were in place—one to each side of the structure. The man in the checked shirt—Deke—was advancing slowly across the yard, taking care to keep a clump of lilac between himself and the bedroom window behind which he'd apparently been told the fugitive was sleeping.

Clucking to the bay, Oliver came about, retraced his steps through the barn and into the passageway between the corrals. There, well hidden by the barn, he went to the saddle, biting back the groan that sprang to his lips when he settled himself and the pressure of his own weight was placed against the wound.

He'd not be able to ride far, he could see that.

46

And if he did much moving about he'd have the wound reopened and bleeding again. Crucita's broth had worked wonders in reviving his strength, but it could do little towards speeding up the natural healing processes of his body.

He moved slowly away from the corrals, allowed his eyes to rove over the surrounding country while he wondered where he might find the greatest safety. He needed time to hole up, allow the leg to rest—and figure out what he should do.

One thing was in his favor: it was not long until dark. The sun had dropped below the hills to the west, was now filling the sky with long streamers of pale gold and orange that tinged the bellies of the clouds with fire. The search would end with night, and he could expect to be left in peace until daylight came once more.

There were brushy hills to the south. The land appeared to be rough, broken. He should have no problem locating an effective hiding place there, he reasoned.

Throwing a final glance toward the Carr house, he sought to locate the men—and Julie. The intervening sheds and a corner of the barn closed off his view. Shrugging, he touched the gelding with his spurs and rode on into the falling darkness.

Chapter *SEVEN*

Shortly Lake Oliver rode down into a fairly wide arroyo that angled toward the hills rising in the southwest. There was little cover, but the depth of the wash was sufficient, and that, combined with the cloak of the steadily gathering night, served to conceal his passage. Thus he gave the problem little thought other than never allowing himself to become silhouetted against the sky.

He felt fairly safe from the men surrounding Carr's ranch house. Undoubtedly they were now closing in. And by the time they discovered he was no longer in Julie's bedroom or elsewhere on the premises, he would be well away from the area. By then darkness would prevent any further search for him.

There were possibilities of encountering one of the remaining posses working the country, however, and he maintained a long-range watch and listened intently for any sounds that would reveal their location. But as the minutes passed he neither heard nor saw any riders, and eventually he was deep in the hills and moving toward a line of bluffs that offered a good place in which to spend the night.

He needed to get off the saddle as soon as

possible, ease the sullen pain that throbbed in his leg. And he wanted to think, to figure out the best course to follow when the time came to make a move.

Reaching the brush-littered buttes, he circled the end, rode the bay to the top. There, pulling back a distance so as to not become etched upon the horizon, he continued on until he found a fairly deep depression along the rim of the formation. Guiding the gelding into it, he halted, dismounted slowly, heaving a sigh of relief.

Pain rocked him as the injured member assumed its share of his weight. He swore deeply, brushed at the sweat that popped out on his face. Grim, jaw clamped shut, he tied the bay to a clump of white-flowered Apache plume and limped to the forward edge of the sink. There he settled down thankfully.

He had picked a good position. Although the distant flat was now in darkness, he would be able to see any who sought to approach the bluffs, and thus be forewarned. Likely Carr's ranch would not be visible because of the trees growing to the south of it, but the dots of light on to the east could only be the settlement.

Sprawled out on the slope of the hollow, as comfortable as could be expected, Lake began to mull over his problems. His first thoughts were to simply ride on, forget San Sabal and the troubles that had risen to plague him.

There was nothing to hold him back; traveling would be painful for a day or two more and then likely would go unnoticed, and the wound, so well carred for by Julie and Crucita, would require no more attention if he was careful.

He had trail grub, enough at least to last for a time, eliminating the need to stop at some town and replenish his stock where he would run the risk of being recognized by some lawman who had been warned of his possible arrival by the committee in San Sabal.

Lake's thoughts came to a dead halt as that scored into his mind. . . . That was the trouble; if he rode on he at once became a wanted man—a hunted killer with two murders hanging over his head.

Lake stirred angrily. Two killings and a bank robbery to his credit and he had no part of any of it! He was guilty in the eyes of all those in San Sabal simply because he had once been convicted of a crime and had served a term in the penitentiary for it.

It was a hell of a thing to think about. He could spend the rest of his life on the run, dodging the law, avoiding towns and people simply because the mistake he had made in the past, and for which he'd already paid the price demanded, now caused him to be tagged a murderer and a bank robber.

There would be no safety anywhere, no peace to be found. The old wanted dodgers that had been issued on him for the stagecoach holdup would be dug out, posted, and this time, because a lawman had died, the efforts to run him down would be doubly intense—and never abandoned. It would be a hopeless way of life.

He squirmed again to lessen the throbbing in his leg and glanced to the east. A late-rising moon was lifting above the horizon, beginning to flood the land with a soft, pale glow. Somewhere behind him a wolf howled, and the bay stamped heavily as he cropped at the bunch grass within his reach.

He could do but one thing—give himself up and take his chances on proving himself innocent. He'd go to Tom McCoy at the White Eagle, hand over his gun to him. Such would be safer than turning himself over to one of the posses. Just how he could then go about proving himself not guilty of the charges against him was not clear; but there had to be a way.

The sharp click of metal against rock carried to him through the night's stillness. He sat up quickly, and rolling over, looked down into the arroyo.

A string of riders were moving along the floor of the wash he had followed after leaving the Carr place. They were almost directly below him, their approach having been muffled by the loose sand. He recognized the man in the lead even in the poor light; Deke—there was no mistaking his checked shirt.

One of the riders said something. The words were inaudible to Lake as the party was still too distant. Whatever it was Deke, his faced tipped down, shook his head in reply.

They had tracked him from Carr's. Oliver realized that in the next moment. After they had discovered he was gone, they had probably spread out. One of them had picked up the prints of the bay where he had moved away from the barn and down into the wash. From there on it would have been easy—up to that moment. Night was undoubtedly making further trailing an impossibility.

Tense, Lake watched the riders draw nearer. If they stayed in the arroyo they would pass immediately below him, not fifty feet away—much too close. The bay had only to shake his head, set up a jingling of bridle metal to draw their attention. Gun in hand, he waited out the moments.

"Might as well give it up, Deke. . . . We've lost him."

"Hell, yes," a second voice chimed in impatiently.

"He could be anywhere—and it's too dang dark to go poking around in the brush."

Deke pulled to a stop. Jerking off his hat, he ran a hand across his face, lifted his eyes to the rim of the buttes and probed their length.

"Reckon you're right. He could've cut off back there a ways, headed west. And these here tracks we been following could be old. Can't tell in this light."

"My hunch is he lined out for Canoncito. It ain't but thirty mile."

Deke shook his head. "Man's pretty bad shot up, according to Carr. Can't see him riding that far. Be more like him to scout hisself up a hole around here, lay out the night, then move on come morning."

"Maybe, but a jasper knowing he's same as dead if he shows his face anywhere in this country ain't going to think much on resting. He's going to be thinking about getting the hell out of here. I figure he's long gone."

Deke again brushed at his face, replaced his hat. "Could be," he admitted wearily. "One thing for damn sure, we ain't doing no good here. Might as well head back to town, get something to eat and a little sleep. We can get back here early, before daylight, see if we can't pick up his trail once more."

"Be smart to bring the rest of the boys now that we got him sort of located. All of us start beating the brush, like as not we'll chase him out."

"Can bring them if they've rounded up the rest of the gang. Don't be forgetting there's three others."

"Guess I was at that. Keep thinking mostly about him—he being the one that cut down the marshal."

"We want 'em all!" Deke said in a taut voice.

"Every goddamned one of them—but important one is this Oliver. Alive if we can take him."

"Something that ain't apt to happen. He knows what he's up against. Can figure on him shooting it out."

"For certain. . . . Come on, let's strike for home —but keep watching sharp. He got the marshal in the back, just as apt to kill any man who gets near him the same way. Thing to do if you spot him is to shoot first—only be damned sure it's him. There's men scattered all over this valley looking for him."

A murmur of agreement and understanding passed through the line as the horses moved out. Tense, Lake Oliver watched them pull off to the left, climb from the arroyo, and head down the slope for the flats and the distant town.

When the last of the dim figures had faded into the silvered night, he rolled back to his original position, one that allowed his injured leg greater comfort, and thought of what he had overheard. One thing was certain in his mind now: he could forget riding in and giving himself up—even to Tom McCoy. He'd never live long enough to face the committee.

Rufe Dillow had been killed from behind, a coward's bullet in his back, and feeling was running so high over that fact alone that a lynching party would be his immediate fate once he came into the reach of the townspeople, while on the other hand, quick death from a bullet would be his finish if he encountered any of the many posses searching for him—assuming he could judge from the words and attitudes of Deke and his men, and there was no reason to doubt them.

But he couldn't—wouldn't—spend the rest of his days as a fugitive running from the law, fearing for his life, wondering if the end lay around the next bend of a trail or some street corner of a distant unknown town. His mind was firmly made up to that.

Canoncito. . . . A settlement thirty miles away. There was his answer. He could ride to it, turn himself over to its marshal, or whatever lawman was in charge, inform him of his predicament. If luck was with him word would not have yet reached the town telling of the killings in San Sabal. He doubted if anyone had paused long enough to send out such messages; all were too busy trying to run him to earth.

It was the only course open to him, the only way he would stand a chance. Abruptly he came to that decision, and pulling himself erect, stared thoughtfully off into the night. It wouldn't be smart to spend the night in the buttes. Deke and his men, plus a few others, would be combing through them by sunup that next morning. It was best he find a different spot, get as far from the area as possible.

Turning, he walked slowly and painfully to the grazing bay. There were trees on to the south. He'd go there, rest for a few more hours, and then head for Canoncito. He should be able to make the settlement with no trouble, as the posses would busy themselves along the bluffs for several hours, and by the time they were ready to give up and look elsewhere he would be out of the valley and well on his way.

Swinging awkwardly onto the saddle, he cut the gelding about and pointed for the darker band that marked the location of the trees.

Chapter *EIGHT*

There was a stream, a small, glinting strip of silver that wound in and out of the oaks and cottonwoods and other growth, and made of the grove a pleasant, friendly place.

Halting beside the quiet water, Oliver allowed the anxious bay to crowd up and slake his thirst in long, noisy draughts while he pulled his blanket roll free of the cantle and dropped it to the ground. He stepped back then, stood for a minute considering the big horse. He should remove the saddle and bridle, picket the gelding properly, but he decided against it. This was hostile country and there was a good possibility he would have to mount up and leave in a hurry. It wouldn't hurt the bay to carry his gear that one night.

Stringing a rope of sufficient length to allow the horse ample grazing as well as access to the creek, Lake spread his tarp-enclosed bedding and stretched out upon it, only then realizing how tired he was. Dillow's bullet had taken more out of him than he'd thought; a few hours' sleep was going to do him a lot of good—but a few hours was all he dare take. He must be up and on his way to Canoncito long before daylight—before the posses from San Sabal began probing the hills and flats again.

Gathering the corner of his blanket, he cast a final glance at the bay, saw that the horse was contentedly munching at the thick grass growing along the stream's bank, and rolled himself into the warmness of the woven wool cover.

It was a mistake. Lake Oliver had not reckoned with the lingering potency of old Crucita's medicated broth, which, coupled with his own jaded physical and mental condition, conspired to provide him with a full night's sound sleep.

He roused abruptly, aware that it was broad daylight, that birds were singing in the trees around him, that the warmness of the sun was already upon the land.

Alarm rocked through him and he bounded to his feet, gasped as pain stabbed through his leg. Ignoring it, he snatched up his bed, quickly rolled it into a compact cylinder, and hurried to where the bay, finally having his fill of grass, was dozing beneath one of the larger trees.

Oliver lashed the blanket roll into place hastily, coiled in the rope that restrained the gelding, and went immediately onto the saddle. He'd halt, brew coffee and perhaps fix a bit of breakfast later on; right now his getting out of the San Sabal country as fast as possible, and unseen, was urgent.

He swung the bay around, and with the distant towering bulk of the mountains at his back, spurred off through the trees.

Minutes later he broke out into the open, headed across a wide strip of sandy ground sparsely populated with clumps of snakeweed, rabbit brush, and other bleached scrubs. To his right he could see the hazy formations that were the buttes where he had hidden earlier.

He was doubly pleased now that he had shown foresight enough to move from that point and find a place some distance away to spend the night. More than likely there was a posse working out the area at that exact moment. Had he been foolish enough to remain there—and oversleep—

Lake Oliver swore deeply at his own carelessness. He should have kept riding, not pulled in for the night at all. He should have kept right on going until he reached Canoncito, bad leg or no. . . . But he hadn't, and there was no use hashing it over now.

He looked ahead to the low, rolling hills bubbling off into the distance from the yonder side of the flat he was crossing. There didn't appear to be much cover on them. Mostly more snakeweed and such low growth. However, the hills themselves would offer protection as long as he remembered to ride the low sides and keep to the swales, always avoiding the summits.

He gained the end of the open ground, breathed deeper. That was the worst of it—the crossing. Twisting about, he looked back. There was no sign of riders. He had attracted no one's attention. Now, all that remained was to make it to Canoncito, turn himself over to the law, and tell his story. He'd be on the way to clearing his name then; to the marshal there it would seem reasonable that, if guilty, he wouldn't have ridden in and given himself up—not with the sanctuary of the Mexican border within reach.

Lake Oliver hauled back sharply on the gelding's reins as alarm burst through him. His hand darted for the pistol at his side as a half a dozen or more riders moved suddenly into view, boxing him in.

"Forget it, Oliver!" a voice lashed at him.

Taut, cursing under his breath, Lake raised his arms slowly. He'd ridden straight into one of the posses. Evidently they had been searching the hills to the west, had spotted him coming, and lain in wait. . . . That night's sleep was liable to cost him his life, he thought bitterly.

"Get his gun. . . . Knife, too, if he's carrying one."

The bearded man in the center of the party who had sung out the warning was well up in years. The cocked rifle he had leveled looked to be new.

One of the riders kneed his horse in close to the bay, approaching carefully from the rear. The others drifted nearer, tightening the circle. Lake felt the lessening of weight against his thigh as his pistol was lifted from its holster.

"I got it, Mr. Mayes."

Mayes. . . . Lake considered the name, tried to recall where he had seen or heard it. It came to him—the owner of the general store; it was on the sign that fronted the building. Maybe he was going to have a bit of luck. Mayes appeared to be a reasonable man, and the riders with him seemed less determined to shoot him on sight or lynch him than had Deke and his party—or the ones who had been with Rufe Dillow.

"Step down," the storekeeper said, motioning with the muzzle of the long gun.

Oliver shifted his weight, came off the bay slowly, not forgetting his injured leg. He hung for a moment, steadying himself by clinging to the saddle and resting his weight against the gelding.

58

"Get back—away from that horse!" Mayes barked, his voice rising with suspicion.

Lake raised both hands, pulled back. Sweat was standing out on his face in large beads, clouding his eyes, but he made no move to brush it aside. The riders, despite the restraining presence of the storekeeper, were edgy, unquestionably trigger-happy.

"Sure him all right," one of the men muttered as the others began to dismount. "Can see where the marshal shot him."

"It's him," Mayes said flatly. "Happens I seen him when he was in town. . . . Gibbs, run your hands over him, be damn sure he ain't packing a hideout gun. Somebody better take a look inside them saddlebags, too. Might have another pistol there."

Gibbs, a large, heavy, leather-tough man, stepped up to Lake, searched his person thoroughly, and turned away.

"Ain't carrying nothing."

"No guns in his saddlebags either," the rider probing the leather pouches on the hull added.

Mayes relaxed, came off his horse in the painful, stiff way of a man forking a horse again after avoiding it for too many months.

"Good," he rumbled. "Now, one of you shake out a rope. Aim to get this jasper back into town for a first class hanging—right out in the middle of the square."

Oliver shrugged, lowered his hands carefully. "It mean anything for me to tell you I didn't shoot Rufe Dillow or that man in the bank? Had nothing to do with any of it."

The rider called Gibbs spat. "Hell, no—won't do you a damned bit of good—you bastard!" he snarled, and whipped the stock of the rifle he carried at Lake's head.

Oliver flung up an arm, blocked the blow. The quick motion caused him to stagger, shift weight to his weak leg. It gave beneath him and he went to one knee. Anger rushed through him. He came up at once, lunged for Gibbs. Mayes moved forward, shouldered him back, and faced Gibbs.

"Be none of that, Harry. Ain't right to rough up a man just because—"

"The hell it ain't!" Gibbs shouted. "Sonofabitch like him ain't got no rights!" Not after what he's done. Ben Carr was a friend of mine—a mighty good one."

Lake Oliver wheeled to the man. "Was? That mean something happened to him?"

Gibb's face flamed a bright red. "Why, goddamn you, standing there asking a question like that! You know what happened!"

Again Mayes stepped in between the two men. He shook his head at Harry Gibbs. "Ease off. Ain't going to help Ben none, blowing off the way you are. Or the marshal and Hilton either. Only way to even up is get him back to town so's the committee can take action. . . . How about that rope?"

Lake felt the coils of the riata drop about him, jerk his arms tight against his sides. Another rider closed in, began to help in winding the rough strands about him. He was barely conscious of it, however. His attention was on Mayes.

"What about Ben Carr?"

The merchant cocked his head to one side, spat. "All right, play dumb if you want. Ain't going to do you no good."

"Not playing dumb. Last time I saw Carr he was standing in his yard with his daughter. One of your posses was surrounding the house. They thought I was inside."

"Only you wasn't," Gibbs broke in. "You was running for the hills. Then you laid for Ben, bushwhacked him when he rode for town last night—"

"Bushwhacked him!" Oliver yelled in exasperation. "That's a damned lie! Why the hell would I want to kill him?"

"Because he put Deke and the others on to where you was hiding, that's why. That girl of his had taken a shine to you, done some doctoring and—"

"Not a word of truth in that," Lake said heavily. "Same as claiming I murdered the marshal and that fellow Hilton. Had nothing to do with any of it. . . . You've got a killer running loose around here."

"We *had*," Mayes corrected pointedly.

"Still have," Lake countered. "I'm not your man. Aim to prove it if I get a chance."

"You'll get it," Mayes said. "Put him on his horse, boys, and let's get started. . . . Best we take the long way around, going back. As soon as not run into any of the others if we can help it. Too many hotheads loose out there and we've got to keep this bird alive long enough for the committee to do its job."

Chapter *NINE*

It was still early when they reached the settlement. Men and women alike were standing around in groups along the street, on the landings fronting the stores. In the square near Garrison's Saddle & Harness Shop, a fairly large crowd had gathered and was listening raptly to a tall, cadaverous man in a dark suit.

"Appears the reverend's hard at it," one of the riders commented as the party crossed over and headed for the alley that would allow them to reach the jail's rear entrance.

Mayes grunted. "Can always depend on him to rile folks up and make things ten times worse."

Lake Oliver, rigid on his saddle, held motionless by the rope that encircled his body and clamped arms to his sides, paid scant attention. Pain was slashing at him with persistent force along with the numbing realization that he was probably living his last moments of life. Earlier his situation had been bad; now, locked in a cell where he would be unable to do anything to clear himself, surrounded by hostile people who wanted only to see him hanged, it was nothing short of hopeless.

They pulled to a halt behind the marshal's office,

dismounted quickly. Mayes opened the door hurriedly, anxious to get his prisoner inside before notice of the capture was taken, while Gibbs, haggard features set, dragged Lake roughly to the landing, shoved him at the door.

Oliver staggered, recovered his balance, and stepped into the low-roofed building. A row of three barred cells lay immediately to his left, on beyond which was a second door that led into the marshal's quarters. No one was there, apparently, as Mayes disappeared into the room, returned at once with a ring of keys. Opening the forward cell, the storekeeper waited while Gibbs and one of the others removed the rope binding Lake. That done, they pushed him into the cubicle and locked the door.

The merchant heaved a deep sigh as he stepped back. "Lucky—that's what we were. Mighty damned lucky."

Harry Gibbs, hands on hips, head thrust forward on his bull neck, glared steadily at Oliver. The hate in his eyes was an unwavering flame.

"Ain't over yet—not by a hell of a lot. Folks hear we got him, they're liable to take things into their own hands. . . . And I'm thinking maybe that ain't such a bad idea. Just hanging's too good for this bastard."

"Maybe, but you can only kill a man once—and we want this done legal by the committee."

"They'd best get a meeting going pretty fast, then."

The store owner bobbed his head briskly. "Probably be this afternoon, after the funerals. Meantime, expect we ought to keep a man standing guard here —round the clock. Amos, get one of them shotguns from the rack and set yourself there in the office where you can keep an eye on the street. Jake—

take a look at that back door, be sure it's locked."

Amos, a squat, dark man with a tobacco-stained beard, shrugged. "Don't hardly see no point in protecting him. I sure ain't going to shoot nobody trying to do what the committee'll do later, anyway."

Mayes inclined his head slightly at the older Amos. "Glad you made yourself clear. Just forget what I said. . . . Earl, you take the watch. I'll see somebody spells you in a couple of hours."

Earl, a much younger man dressed in a gray business suit, said, "All right, Mr. Mayes," and moved toward the connecting doorway. He hesitated, looked back over his shoulder uncertainly. "What'll I do if people start ganging up ouside?"

"Point your scattergun at the sky and fire off a warning shot. That'll make them think for a minute or two, and give the rest of us time to get here."

Lake, sitting on the hard cot at the back of his cell, easing the pain that throbbed in his leg, watched the men file out and disappear into the street. Earl dragged up a chair, placed it advantageously where he could see both the cells and the area fronting the jail, and sat down, shotgun across his knees.

There was no one visible beyond the building's entrance, but Oliver knew such would not hold for long. He could hear a low rumble of voices coming from somewhere close, guessed word was already spreading despite Mayes's hope to keep the news of his capture quiet.

Rising, Lake crossed slowly to the window of his cell and looked out. The groups and clusters of townspeople he had noted when they rode in were increasing, growing larger. Eventually they would fuse, become a single mob. He shook his head, and turning back, placed his attention on Earl.

"There a lawyer in this town I can talk to?"

The younger man stirred. "Got a couple around. Doubt if either one'll be interested in listening to you."

"Like to see one, anyway. Any chance of you getting word to them?"

"Maybe. Can't go myself. If somebody drops by I'll see if they'll do it for you."

A thought came to Lake. Tom McCoy at the White Eagle would be a good man to speak with. He could at least learn the details of what had happened, get a clear picture of what he was supposed to have done. The saloonman had seemed friendly enough.

"How about McCoy? Mind sending for him, too?"

Earl shifted, came half around on his chair. "McCoy? He a friend of yours?"

"About as near to a friend as I've been able to make in this town. Only met him yesterday."

"Then why—"

"Take him to be a reasonable man. Figure I can talk to him."

Earl shrugged. "Speaking of a reasonable man, you better be glad it was Mayes that caught up with you and not some of the others. You'd a been swinging from a tree right now, most likely."

"Can' see as it'll make much difference whether this committee I keep hearing about does it, or some lynch mob. All the same. And Mayes—seems he just wants to be sure the committee says it's all right. He's got his mind made up about me same as all the rest."

"Not much doubt, far as I can see. Everything points to you.

"Points, maybe, but that's where it ends. I had nothing to do with the killings or the robbery."

65

"You prove it?"

"How the hell can I—locked up in this cell?"

Earl fell silent. Heat was beginning to rise in the small, boxlike rooms. Propping his weapon against the doorframe, he rose, removed his coat. Draping it over the back of his chair, he sat down again, took up the shotgun, and resumed his position.

"You'll be getting your chance to talk before the committee. It'll be the same as a trial."

"My talking and their listening will be two different things. They ever let a man go that was brought up before them?"

"Well—no. Usually was a deal where everybody was sure—"

"And punishing a man—it ever anything but hanging?"

"No, can't say it was—"

"What I figured. Your committee's not a judge and a jury—they're hangmen, and somebody hauled up to face them guilty or not's got about as much chance as the devil in church."

A party of riders swept into the street, pounded for some point farther down. . . . One of the posses returning, Oliver guessed. They'd all be coming in now; like as not a messenger was seeking out the different groups at that moment, advising them of the capture. He wondered about the outlaws—his gang, as they'd been called—who were involved in the bank holdup and murder.

"See there's nobody else locked up in here. That mean they haven't found the men who killed Hilton?"

"Not yet," Earl replied without turning. "But we will. Everything's going to stop now, however, for the funerals."

Boot heels rapped on the boardwalk outside. Earl

66

straightened, lifted the shotgun, pointed its twin muzzles at the doorway. A moment later Russ Sadilek, accompanied by two men, entered. The clothing of the tall, onetime rancher was rumpled, dusty from riding. His features betrayed his weariness.

He bucked his head crisply at the young guard, glanced at Oliver. "Finally got him. That's good. Any word yet on the rest of the bunch?"

"Not yet," Earl replied.

Lake moved up against the bars, faced the man. "Like to talk with Tom McCoy. Mind passing that on to him?"

Sadilek became thoughtful. "What can he do for you?"

"Nothing, maybe, but I'm needing help from somebody."

"Friend, you're needing a lot of help!" one of the men with Sadilek said, and laughed.

"Oh, he's going to get some help—walking up to the gallows," the other added.

Russ Sadilek rubbed at his jaw. A voice down the street was yelling, but the words were unintelligible.

"Suppose there's no harm in it," he said slowly. "What makes you think Tom'll come?"

"Don't know that he will. Only asking."

The tall man's shoulders stirred. "Well, we'll see," he said indifferently, and swung about to Earl. "Expect you'll be wanting to attend the services, seeing as how you worked for Ed Hilton. Got somebody coming to relieve you?"

"Mr. Mayes said he'd send a man. Reckon I'd best wait for him."

"Suit yourself," Sadilek said, moving toward the door. "Keep your eyes open now. Crowd's starting to get ugly. That damned preacher's working them

67

up good, spouting his eye-for-an-eye pap. . . . All hell's liable to bust loose around here."

"Can bet on it," one of his companions said. "Only I don't figure it'll come until after the buryings."

Sadilek said, "Way I see it—and by then we'll be ready."

Oliver wiped at the sweat on his face with a forearm, remained silent as the three left the building. More riders came in, a large party this time, judging from the sound of the hooves. Probably three or four of the posses.

A bell began to toll slowly. Earl got to his feet, moved to the doorway, and looked anxiously toward Mayes's store. Somewhere in the distance a gunshot flatted across the still, hot air.

Lake returned to his cot and sat down, taking the pressure off his wounded leg. His belt, holster empty, was yet around his waist, and he started to remove it, thought better of the idea. Mayes and his posse members, thanks to inexperience in such matters, had taken only his pistol, neglected to also remove the leather strap, heavy with cartridges. He'd keep it on; it might prove an asset if the opportunity for escape presented itself.

And escape he must if he was to avoid hanging either at the hands of the town's committee or a lynch mob. He was done for either way unless he could somehow prove his innocence.

A lawyer might be able to help—just as there was some possibility Tom McCoy could do him a service. But he couldn't bank on the saloonman being willing to stand by him any more than he could force one of the town's lawyers to defend him. What would be done, he'd have to do himself. But what?

How could he find the killer—or killers? Where could he start?

Julie Carr. . . .

He hadn't thought of her. There was a chance Ben had said something to her before he died that would help—that would give him something to go on. *If she would talk to him;* that was the catch there. Likely, she, too, was convinced, as was everyone else in San Sabal, that he had killed her father out of revenge.

He mulled the problem about in his mind. Asking her to come to him at the jail would be useless. He'd have to go to her, force himself upon her if necessary. It became clearer as he considered it that she was his one hope.

The bell had ceased its tolling. Earl, still in the doorway, swore softly, and then he pulled back, a smile of relief on his face. Boots thumped again on the sidewalk and shortly the entrance was filled as Cal Jessup stepped in.

"Glad you got here," Earl said, thrusting the shotgun into his hands. "I'm going to be late for the services."

The deputy stared at him for a moment, nodded. "Better get moving, then," he said, and stepped aside.

Earl immediately snatched up his coat and bolted into the street, heading for the opposite end of town. As the sound of his running steps died, Jessup turned to Lake. Standing the shotgun against the wall, he walked slowly to the cell, a half grin on his thin lips.

"Well, killer, how's it feel in there? Reckon it ain't nothing new to you, howsomever, looking through bars."

Oliver eyed the man coldly. With the entire town

69

gathered at the church for the funeral services of its banker and marshal, there would be no better time for a try at escaping. The problem was how to pull it off. Silent, he stared at the lawman.

Jessup drew a cigar from his pocket, bit off the end, spat it into a corner. "One thing you can sure bank on, you won't be looking through them here long as you did in the pen. The committee's planning to meet this evening. Means you'll be swinging before noon tomorrow." The deputy paused, a match halfway to his cigar. A frown clouded his brow.

"Why, them dumb cowhands—you're still wearing your gunbelt!"

Lake continued to watch the lawman. The deputy tossed aside the match, reached for the ring of keys lying on a nearby desk, and moved to the door.

"Turn yourself around—back up to me," he ordered.

Oliver complied slowly, indifferently. He heard the key rattle in the lock, the dull click as it flipped back the tumbler. There was a creaking then as the grill was opened.

"Got my gun on you," Jessup warned. "Make one bad move and I'll blow you in two. . . . Now, I want you to unbuckle that belt, pass it back real careful like over your shoulder to me. Understand?"

Tense, nerves cool, Lake Oliver nodded. His fingers sought the tongue of the buckle, pressed while he pulled the end of the thick leather strap, freed it.

"Watch yourself," the deputy said sharply. "Like I told you—got my gun on you! As soon shoot—"

"Know you would," Lake drawled, and started to raise his arm, hand the belt back as Jessup had directed. "Here—take it!"

70

In a swift lunge, Oliver rocked to one side, swung the belt in a hard, short arc. Jessup's pistol blasted into the heated quiet of the room as the strap, heavy with its row of neatly looped brass and lead cartridges, smashed into the side of the man's head.

Lake felt the bullet sear across his shoulder, leave its quick, stinging burn, heard it thud into the wall beyond him as he came fully around.

Chapter *TEN*

Luke was certain there was no one within hearing distance of the gunshot, but he nevertheless stepped over the deputy's prone shape, crossed to the door, and looked into the street. It appeared everyone in San Sabal was at the church.

He moved back to Jessup. The cartridge belt had proved to be an effective weapon. The lawman lay face down on the dusty floor. He was out cold, and an oblong-shaped welt, darkening rapidly, extended from the point of his jaw to the temple on the left side of his head. Kicking the dropped pistol out of the cell, Lake caught Jessup under the armpits and boosted him onto the cot.

Turning back into the office, he located a pair of handcuffs, linked the deputy's wrists behind him with the steel manacles, then, using a bandanna, gagged him tightly. That done, he stepped from the cell, pulled the door shut and locked it. Services at the church and later at the cemetery would likely consume another hour, and he doubted if anyone would drop by the jail before such were concluded. He guessed he wasn't too pressed for time.

Buckling on his belt, he recovered his forty-five from the marshal's desk and crossed to the back door. He had no exact idea where his horse would be—in one of the stables, he assumed, recalling that he'd heard Mayes tell someone to send a hostler for the animals. It would be a matter of visiting each barn until he found the bay.

He'd get the horse, head out fast for the Carr ranch, talk with Julie, he decided as he let himself out into the alley. She wouldn't have come in for the funerals, having her own grief to shoulder. He pulled up short, surprise and satisfaction coming over him. The bay, along with the rest of the posse horses, was still at the rack behind the building.

Someone had failed to notify the hostler—or else the man was simply waiting until after the burial services were over to attend to the chore. That probably was the answer. . . . Not that it mattered to Lake. It simplified things greatly for him.

Limping badly, he moved up to the bay, and jerking the leathers free, went to the saddle. He sat there for a few moments, wishing he might talk with Tom McCoy before he rode out. Julie would be able to supply information only concerning the death of her father. The saloonman could pretty well fill him in on all of it—the murder of Hilton, of Marshal Rufe Dillow, and of the rancher.

There would be things he'd know that the girl would be unaware of, and such fragments, put together with what Julie could tell him, just might add up to some answers.

But McCoy would be at the funerals, and by the time he returned to his place of business, the rest of San Sabal would be milling in the street, possibly bent on breaking him out of jail and exacting justice then and there. Lake grinned wryly; he could be certain of that when they discovered the deputy gagged and locked in one of the cells.

The posses would hit the saddle again, go racing off into the flats and into the hills determined to run him down. . . . A stillness came over Lake Oliver. Maybe that would be in his favor; they would all expect him to seek safety in flight—why wouldn't it be smarter to do just the opposite and stay right in town?

Immediately he brought the gelding about, and dropping back to the fringe of trees growing along the east side of the settlement, followed it to its end. There he crossed to the opposite side, spurring the bay to a quick run, and doubled back in behind the buildings on that side of the street until he was in the rear of McCoy's White Eagle.

Halting, he looked around for a place to leave the gelding, one where the animal would be quickly available yet go unnoticed. A small barn from which the distinct smell of milk cows originated stood a dozen strides away. At once Lake rode the bay to the rear of the weathered structure and dismounted.

Pulling back the sagging door, he led the gelding into the dark interior, fortunately empty, tied him to one of the milking rings mounted in the wall. The bay wasn't pleased with his surroundings but Oliver got him some water, and spotting a bucket of grain hanging on a peg in one corner, placed it before the horse and he settled down.

Returning to the alley, Lake glanced up and down its length, assured himself that it was still deserted, then hurried to the saloon's rear entrance. Trying the knob, he found it locked. Cursing softly, he glanced to the window a few steps farther along. It was partly open. Moving to it, he raised it the remainder of the way. It took a bit of painful managing with his stiff and tender leg, but eventually he worked himself through and gained an entry.

He was in a small room used by McCoy as an office. There was a makeshift desk littered with papers. A half a dozen chairs were placed about, and against one wall was a large coatrack. Lake crossed to the door in the opposite wall, drew it open carefully. It led into a short hall at the end of which was the main part of the saloon. He could see the end of the bar from where he stood.

The building was deserted, eerie in its smoky, dimly lit silence. Oliver stepped in behind the counter, treated himself to a stiff drink, and returned to the office. He could think of no better place to wait for the saloonman than there. The only thing he'd have to worry about was if McCoy, who probably would go straight to his office when he came in, would be alone. Having one or several men with him would create complications.

Anticipating such, Oliver glanced around the room. Another door in the wall to the right of the window took his attention. Opening it cautiously, he peered out. It led into a narrow passageway that lay between the saloon and the adjoining building— the Cattle Queen Hotel, Lake thought, but wasn't sure. It evidently was a sort of private entrance. That was good; a man leaving the White Eagle by such a route could avoid both the alley and the street, if the need arose.

He came back around. He still hadn't found a place where he could remain out of sight if McCoy had others with him when he entered. His glance fell on the coatrack. High, a yard or more in width, it supported several items of clothing that formed an effective curtain. It would serve the purpose admirably.

75

Moving it out a bit from the wall but otherwise not changing its location, Lake stepped in behind it. He would go unseen there while enjoying a full view of the room. Too, the door to the side passageway was only a long step away; if he had to leave fast he could do so.

Satisfied, he went again into the saloon proper, once more measured himself a drink. The liquor seemed to help, not only allaying to some extent the steady, dull pain in his leg but easing the tension that gripped him.

The services should be over. They had already begun when Cal Jessup had arrived at the jail to relieve Earl, and better than a half hour had elapsed since then. Thinking it over, he reckoned it would be closer to a full hour. He guessed he'd better get himself set. McCoy just might take it on himself to use the side door rather than the front, and he could find himself trapped and unable to reach his hiding place.

Moving into the office, Oliver stepped in behind the rack, leaned against the wall to take the weight off his leg. The church bell began to ring again, a lonely, spaced beat that seemed to bespeak the emptiness of death, and Lake realized the funerals were over at last.

Abruptly taut, he drew his pistol, checked the cylinder to be certain it was fully loaded. McCoy, he hoped, would prove cooperative—or at least not too hostile to talk. There was no way of knowing; the saloonman had been friendly enough at the start, but things had changed since then. He now stood accused—and convicted—of three murders, and Tom McCoy could be going right along with the rest of San Sabal in believing such.

It all depended upon how open-minded the man

was. If like all the others he was inclined to jump to conclusions, base his thinking on the past, and upon evidence that wasn't evidence at all but pure assumption, then he'd get no help at all from the man. But McCoy didn't appear to have that turn of mind. He seemed—

Lake Oliver drew himself up stiffly as a key rattled in the double doors overlapping the bat-wings at the saloon's front entrance. McCoy had returned. Pistol again in his hand, Oliver waited.

Chapter *ELEVEN*

The saloonman was not using the side entrance. That simplified matters considerably. It was now possible to see immediately if he had others with him or not.

Lake edged from behind the rack, and flat against the wall, made his way to the door. Removing his hat, he peered around the frame. A flood of sunlight suddenly spilled into the murky room as the solid doors were flung back and hooked into place. A moment later the batwings swung in.

Oliver drew taut. A half a dozen or so men trailed McCoy. Pulling off his dark coat, the saloonman gestured at the bar.

"Belly up, gentlemen. I'll be with you soon's I've shucked these churchgoing duds."

Oliver dropped back in behind the rack. Pistol ready, he waited, scarcely breathing. McCoy's boot heels thumped across the bare floor. Moments later he was in the office. Lake watched him pull off his string tie, the celluloid collar, heard him sigh gustily as he hung them on the rack with the coat. He then hooked thumbs under his suspenders, slipped them over his shoulders, and stepped out of the woolen trousers he'd donned for the occasion.

"It all right if I do some bartending, Tom?" a voice called from the saloon.

"Go ahead," McCoy replied. "Be there myself quick as I can climb into some cool clothes," he added, and turned to the rack.

Lake Oliver stepped from behind the hanging clothes. He had no way of knowing how the saloon-man would react, and he could take no chances.

Pistol leveled, he said softly, "McCoy—"

The bar owner pulled up short, features blanked by alarm. "You!"

"Me," Oliver said in a quiet voice. "Mind closing that door?"

McCoy hesitated briefly; then, taking a step forward, caught the panel by its edge and pushed it shut, never removing his sharp eyes from Lake.

"What now? You here to kill me, too?"

Oliver studied the man coldly. He shook his head. "Figured you different from the others. You really think that, then sing out for help," he said, and dropped the forty-five back into its holster.

McCoy stared. "Then what—why—"

"Looking for help—information," Lake said, leaning against the wall again to rest his leg. "Wasn't me that did those killings—none of them. Trying to prove it."

McCoy reached for a pair of light duck pants on the rack, began to draw them on.

"Mayes said he had you locked in a cell. You kill somebody getting out?"

"No. Laid out your deputy, that's all. He'll have a sore head but he'll be all right. . . . There anything you can tell me that might put me on the track of the killer?"

McCoy, again dressed, folded his arms across his chest, continued to stare at Lake. It was as if he found it hard to believe his own eyes. Finally, he wagged his head.

"Expect you know as much about it all as I do. Maybe more."

Lake swore. "All I know is that I'm about to get lynched because I served time in the pen. That—and the fact that I'm riding a bay horse."

"Witnesses seem plenty sure it was your animal, and that you were on it."

"They're dead wrong—either lying or guessing if they claim they recognized me. Hell, there's a lot of bays around."

"Yeh," McCoy said. "Sadilek's got one. The marshal had one, too."

Lake shrugged. "Expect we could spot a few more if we'd look, along with plenty that could pass for bays at night." He paused, suddenly remembering. "You see Sadilek at the funerals?"

McCoy nodded. "Was setting behind me in church, and we walked together going to the grave-yard. Why?"

"He say I asked him to tell you I wanted to see you?"

The saloonman frowned, rubbed at his chin. "No, sure didn't. We were talking about you, too. Was him that said Mayes and his posse had caught you, put you in a cell."

Faint suspicion began to stir through Lake. "Sort of funny. Said he'd tell you."

"Could've forgot—slipped his mind."

"Forgot, hell! How could he when you were talking about me?"

McCoy moved back, sat down on the edge of the table, features drawn into a dark study.

"What about Sadilek?" Oliver continued, allowing his thoughts to ramble on. "He was going up against Rufe Dillow for the marshal's job—and there's that talk about his money petering out. You come to think on it, he's a man with plenty of reason to rob a bank and get rid of the only opposition he has for that star."

The saloonman wagged his head unbelievingly. "No—not Russ Sadilek. . . . Couldn't be. I'll admit he's got the two big reasons but I don't think—"

"I've got to think it—of him and anybody else that's got cause. Hell, it's my neck they're wanting to stretch, and I sure never did any of it. Not the bank robbing or the killings." Lake paused, considered McCoy with a level stare. "There any doubt in your mind about that?"

The saloonman stirred. "Going to be honest and say I was stringing along with the others. But now, your coming here facing me's got me looking at it different. Either you didn't do it or you've got one hell of a lot of guts."

"I didn't do it," Oliver said again, flatly. "What about the others in the robbery, and Hilton's murder? Seems they've not been caught yet."

"So far. Expect everybody was so busy hunting you because of the marshal's death they've plain let that part of it slide."

"What I figured. Would help some if one of those posses would run them down. Could be one of them would talk, clear me."

"A chance, but hell of it is, they're likely halfway to Mexico by now."

Lake didn't have to be told that; it had come to him before. He shifted wearily, moved toward the side entrance to the room.

"Nothing much you can tell me then that'll help, I take it?"

"Wish I could," McCoy replied, coming to his feet. "But like I said, you know much as I do, and—" He broke off suddenly as a shout sounded in the saloon.

Steps pounded across the floor. The saloonkeeper motioned at the rack. Lake recrossed hurriedly, stepped in behind it as the door flew open.

"That killer—he's loose again!" a man cried. "Hostler found Jessup all beat up and locked in one of the jail cells. We're mounting posses now!"

McCoy nodded. "All right, Fitch, I'll be with you in a couple of minutes."

The rider wheeled about, answering questions thrown at him by the men standing at the bar as he hurried on for the batwings. McCoy pushed the door shut again, turned his attention to Lake, once more heading for the side entrance.

"You won't stand much of a chance out there— not with the hills crawling with posses again. This time they'll shoot on sight. Was a fool thing coming here."

Oliver's face was impassive. "Had to find out what I could do. Figured you'd be the one man who'd talk. . . . I'll make out all right."

"Yeh, expect you will. Got any idea what you'll do next?"

"One thing—keep trying to clear my name. Was on my way to Canoncito to give myself up there when I bumped into Mayes and his bunch. I've got no trust in this hanging committee of yours. May have to do that yet if I'm to get a fair shake."

"Probably the smartest thing you can do. Sure be the safest. Tell you this, I'll ask some questions and do a lot of listening, see if I can turn up something that'll maybe help."

"Be obliged to you," Lake said, grasping the doorknob. "Like to know more about Sadilek. Can't keep from getting a feeling about him."

"Do what I can, but I sure think you're trying to tree the wrong possum. Russ wanted Dillow's job, that's for certain, and I expect he's needing cash. Some of the things he invested in didn't exactly pan out, I've heard, but I still figure he ain't the kind to kill a man—not for anything."

Lake's mouth pulled into a hard smile. "Surprise you what a man'll do sometimes when he's been backed into a corner. . . . So long."

McCoy lifted his hand suddenly. "Wait! Where can I reach you in case I turn up something important?"

Oliver considered the saloon owner quietly. "I'll keep in touch with you," he said, and opened the door.

Glancing to both ends of the passageway and finding it clear, he stepped into the open and crossed quickly to the cowshed. He could hear the posses forming in the street less than fifty steps away.

Chapter *TWELVE*

He had delayed almost too long. The shouting and pounding of running feet in the street increased as he jerked the bay's rope free of the ring. Lake paused. It would be dangerous to use the alley; he'd best find a different route.

Turning from the sagging door through which he had entered, he led the gelding out into a littered yard on the opposite side. The band of trees a fair distance to the west of the settlement was his one hope for quick concealment. Once there in the grove, he could double back and ride to the Carr ranch.

Reaching the trees, however, could be a problem and prove his undoing—particularly if his trust in Tom McCoy was misplaced. If the saloonman elected to advise the posse members of his presence, he could expect riders to come swarming into the area any moment.

Jaw set, Oliver again looked toward the trees. . . . If they did come, they'd not find him there waiting. Beyond the yard lay an open field, once plowed and cultivated, now fallow in the bright sunlight. A house stood near its far end, beyond which was another neglected field and then the grove. Lake cast a glance at the rear facade of the White Eagle and the buildings adjoining it; there was no activity there yet, and none at the ends of the alley.

He'd be a fool to spend any more time thinking—best just to chance it. Stepping around to the right-hand side of the bay, thus putting the horse between himself and the settlement, he crossed the yard through the canted gate and entered the field.

A hammering of hooves along the street slowed his step, told him the posses were beginning to move out—that his hope of reaching the grove was decreasing with each passing moment. Grim, he continued, praying he would appear to be just what he was—a man leading a horse through a forgotten field.

He drew abreast the house. Immediately a dog rushed forth from the shade of several withered bushes growing along its west side, raced toward him barking furiously. The bay shied nervously, but Oliver ignored the mongrel, pressed on.

Movement on the porch of the house caught the corner of his eye. Lake's fingers drifted slowly to his gun. It was an elderly man, bearded and with a stringy, unkempt mustache. He walked haltingly to the edge of the sagging gallery, shaded his eyes with a hand and squinted at Oliver. His features were angry.

"You making yourself a road across my land, mister?"

Oliver forced a smile. "Nope. Just taking a short-cut."

"Well, I ain't obliged to you. First thing you know everybody'll be doing it."

Lake continued to smile. The oldster hadn't recognized him—which was understandable. Few persons in San Sabal had actually seen him.

"I'm begging your pardon, friend. Didn't aim to be trespassing. I sure won't do it again."

The old man hawked, spat, brushed at his beard. "See't you don't," he said grumpily, and yelling at the dog, turned back for the rocking chair he had been occupying.

The mongrel refused the command, followed Lake and the gelding to the edge of the trees yapping every step of the way before he finally wheeled and trotted back to the house.

Oliver did not halt until he was well within the cottonwoods and oaks, and entirely hidden from the settlement. He went to the saddle then, sat for a moment head down, waiting for the pain in his leg to subside. Finally, swiping at the sweat gathered on his face, he looked in the direction of San Sabal. There had been no pursuit; either Tom McCoy was being honest with him and had not betrayed his presence to the posses, or by cutting across the fields he had simply gotten away before they could act.

At any rate he was safe—so far. He no longer could hear the sounds along the street, but he could see its upper and lower ends. As he watched, two parties of riders departed, one moving south, the other taking the opposite direction. He sighed heavily, shifted his position on the saddle; chances were that there were already a half a dozen or more such groups searching the country for him. He'd need luck to get out of the grove.

Touching the gelding with his rowels, he moved deeper into the trees, keeping to the shadows as much as possible. It was getting near midday, however, and with a strong sun bearing down from a cloudless sky, there were few large pools of shade to rely upon. Again brushing at the sweat on his face, he looked ahead. Carr's would lie to the west and north; if the grove extended far enough, he could probably get fairly close to the ranch. He hoped so; a solitary rider moving across open country would be spotted quickly by someone.

A time later he saw the edge of the grove in the distance and pulled to a stop. The trees had favored him, forming a long if somewhat narrow finger that extended for several miles along the floor of a broad, shallow valley.

He was surprised that he had encountered no one during the passage, could only explain it by thinking the posses had definite ideas, from some source or reason, as to where he had gone. The parties he'd seen had all taken out for either the north or south, none pointing into the west.

There could be a plan involved, he realized as he considered it. The riders could be figuring to make a wide circle and then turn, form a skirmish line, and work toward the settlement, hoping to flush him out and drive him before them. It would work, too, he thought grimly. If the men undertook such a plan at that moment they would have him trapped between themselves and the town. . . . It could be they were certain he had fled into the grove, either having noticed him—or having been advised of the fact.

It made sense—and it made one thing clear to Lake Oliver; he'd best get out of the trees as fast as possible. It was entirely possible that it was no more than an idea in his own head, had not occurred to the posse members at all, but it was logical, and when his own life was at stake, he could not afford to ignore it.

Swerving the gelding to the left, he continued steadily. He would make use of the trees as long as he could, narrow the time he would be compelled to be in the open as much as he could. Carr's ranch shouldn't be too far.

Abruptly he came to a halt, vague motion along the fringe of the grove arresting him instantly. Riders. Two men. A tautness gripped Lake Oliver. He'd been right about the posses—they were moving into the trees.

Nudging the bay gently, he headed the big horse in behind a clump of mock orange, again stopped. A stillness lay over the grove. Even the insects had ceased their noisy clacking, silenced by the presence of men.

The two riders were working slowly inward. One appeared familiar. It was Harry Gibbs, Lake saw a few moments later—the one who had claimed to be a friend of Ben Carr and who had roughed him up some while he was being brought in by the store-keeper, Mayes. Lake scanned the area to either side of the pair, searching for the remainder of the posse. He could locate no others. Evidently Gibbs and the man with him had split off from the others and were somewhat in advance.

Reaching down, Oliver drew his pistol. He'd make use of it only as a threat, if at all possible; to fire it or allow Gibbs and his partner to trigger theirs would prove fatal; the reports would bring in members of all the posses within hearing distance in short order.

Motionless, he watched the riders approach. Harry Gibbs was a short distance to one side, would pass the clump of orange below him. If the other man maintained his present course, he would move by not much more than an arm's reach away. Fortunately the mock orange was squat and densely leafed. With luck both riders would fail to see him.

If not—if they saw him—Lake tightened his grip

on his weapon. He'd have no choice but to shoot, to fight it out and then try to elude the others who would close in fast. He was a dead man if he offered no resistance. They'd never let him surrender, and while the thought of killing a man—two possibly— did not set with him, they would give him no choice.

"I'm beginning to think your hunch was wrong."

It was Gibbs's partner, a slightly built man cradling a shotgun in his arms.

"Keep your shirt on, Anse. Makes sense that he'd duck into here. Thing he'd been hunting is cover. Grove's the only place close."

"What about them trees on the other side of town?"

"Time when he got loose was while we was all at the graveyard. Somebody'd seen him crossing that flat." Gibbs swore impatiently. "Knowed we should've strung him up when we first grabbed him, but that goddam Mayes—he had to wait and stand him up before the committee. . . . And then Jessup goes and lets him get away—"

"Deputy says it was your fault—your bunch, I mean," Anse countered. "Shouldn't have let him keep wearing his belt."

Gibbs cursed again. "Maybe it was a mistake. Just nobody thought about it. Anyway, a good deputy could've took it from him without getting hisself clobbered."

Oliver tensed. Anse had reached the edge of the mock orange. Farther over, Harry Gibbs had already drawn abreast, was passing. Lake shifted the pistol in his hand, gripped it by the barrel. Employing it as a club depended entirely upon the man being within reach.

Abruptly Anse was there. He was staring moodily

ahead, face empty as his horse plodded stolidly on. For a breath of time Lake thought he was to go unnoticed, and then the rider glanced toward him. His mouth gaped. His eyes spread with surprise— and fear.

In the next instant Oliver spurred forward. He brought the pistol down in a swift arc. The handle thudded against the man's skull—but only partly checked the yell that sprang from his lips.

Lake heard Gibbs's answering shout as he spurred away. A gun blasted through the heat, and twisting, he saw the older man wheeling for him, ignoring Anse, who was falling from his saddle.

Oliver whipped up his own weapon, triggered a shot at the oncoming Gibbs. The man jolted as the bullet smashed into him. Taut, Lake roweled the bay into a fast lope. There'd be hell to pay now.

Chapter *THIRTEEN*

He drove hard for the end of the grove, not sure what he would find when he reached that point— or what he should then do. Somewhere in the distance he heard a shout. Instantly he swerved in behind a stand of mountain mahogany, halted.

A dozen men, all riding fast for the grove. . . . Most were coming across the flat that lay west of the grove. A smaller group was approaching from the south—as had been Gibbs and Anse. There could be no doubt that it was the shooting that had summoned them.

Lake placed his attention on the riders in front of him. Those on the flat were no serious threat at the moment; they would reach the trees well after he had ₚassed, if all went well, but the smaller party was a different matter. Where they were concerned he could be faced with the same problem as Gibbs and his friend with the shotgun had posed— a head-on encounter.

Cautious, he put the gelding to a slow walk, angling to his right, hopeful of finding an avenue of escape in the space between the smaller three-man group and the dozen or more sweeping in from the west. Lake Oliver had tasted enough gunplay and violence, wanted to avoid any further clash if possible.

Innocent of the crimes they sought him for, he now was actually guilty of shooting Harry Gibbs and bashing in his partner's head. Anse likely was not badly hurt, but Gibbs—The man had buckled as if seriously wounded. . . . He could be dead.

Lake swore helplessly. He was getting in deeper with each passing moment. Unless he turned up something soon that would clear his name, he stood a good chance of actually—

He drew the bay in sharply, pivoted fast, and rode into a thicket of brush. A rider had separated from the main party, was cutting away at right angles. Evidently he meant to intercept the smaller group. Likely he was carrying a message or instructions of some sort.

Deep in the undergrowth, Oliver watched the man gallop by a hundred yards in front of him. He recognized the rider as he passed through a sunlit patch of open ground. It was Cal Jessup.

The deputy, a bandage wrapped about his head, was bent low over the saddle. When he came within hailing distance of the three men, he raised an arm and yelled. All altered course, veered toward him.

The moment was opportune for Oliver. For the time the four men were faced from him, Jessup pointing into the grove while the others listened intently. A plan was in the making, it would seem.

Lake wasted no time speculating. Touching the bay with his spurs, he moved out at a fast walk for the edge of the grove, now less than a hundred yards distant. Quickly reaching there, he halted just within the fringe, turned his attention to the deputy and the posse members with him.

They had resumed, were spreading out as they

entered the trees. Oliver sighed with relief. He was behind them now, and beyond the men coming in from the west. He need worry no longer about either party, had only to be on the alert for other posses.

He stalled out several minutes there just within the trees, allowing time for Jessup and the rest to get well into the grove, and then once more roweling the bay, headed across the flat for Carr's ranch.

The place was quiet as he entered the yard, choosing to avoid the front and approach from the side he had employed when escaping that evening before. Shortly he heard voices, low-pitched and near, and pulled to stop. Dismounting, he tied the gelding behind a tamarisk windbreak, and made his way along the side of the house until he reached the corner.

A buckboard and a red-wheeled surrey were drawn up to the hitchrack. Three couples, all elderly, were walking slowly from the porch where Julie, in company with Crucita, was standing. . . . Neighbors paying their respects, Lake realized. Likely they had just buried Ben Carr. Julie would have put him in the family plot somewhere on the ranch.

He watched the couples climb into their vehicles, heard them repeat their condolences and express their final comforting reassurances, and saw them move on.

It was a hell of a time to confront Julie Carr with questions, but he couldn't wait. The posse members in the grove would be on the move again soon—perhaps already were—doubly determined now after finding Harry Gibbs and Anse. Every minute was precious.

"Now you will sleep. . . ." Crucita's words were low, insistent.

The girl nodded woodenly. "For a while," she murmured.

Lake wheeled at once, forgetting his injured leg, swearing softly as it gave under the sudden movement. Disregarding the pain, he hurried back along the side of the house to the window he had used before. It was still open. Moving fast, he climbed through into the room. Julie would come there for her nap—he hoped.

Brushing away sweat from his face, he crowded into a corner, hiding himself behind a chair upon which a robe of some sort had been thrown, and waited. Within moments the girl appeared. Her features were drawn, eyes heavy. She crossed to the bed, sat down, and hands clasped in her lap, stared vacantly at the floor.

"Julie—"

At Lake Oliver's quiet voice she came to her feet. Her eyes flared and a cry leaped to her lips. He was upon her in a long stride, clamping one hand over her mouth, holding her tightly with an arm.

"Don't," he said in a whisper. "Just want to talk to you, that's all. . . . Ask some questions."

She remained rigid, unyielding, pressed against him.

"Not aiming to hurt you—or anybody. And I didn't kill your pa. None of the others, either. . . . That's what I'm here for—trying to clear up my name. Will you let me talk?"

She was motionless for a time, then moved her head in agreement. He released her, pushed her gently back onto the bed. Turning, he closed the door that led into the rest of the house, thus excluding Crucita or any others of the hired help who might overhear.

"Want to say I'm sorry about your pa," he began, pulling up the chair and sitting before her.

Julie stared at him, hostility still in her eyes, lips pulled to a firm line. He sighed.

"I'll tell you again—I wasn't the one who shot your pa. Never saw him again after I ducked out that window and gave that posse the slip. You and he were standing out there in the yard watching them when I rode off."

Her expression did not change. He was having no success with her. After a moment he shrugged wearily. "Can see this is just a waste of time— coming here. But I figured you might help."

"Help!" she echoed bitterly, coming alive suddenly. "You're the last man in this world I'd ever help!"

"Why—because you think I ambushed your pa?"

"That's exactly why! Just because he did what he thought was right, told those men—"

"I never killed him," Oliver repeated doggedly. "How many times do I have to say it? Hell—use your head! Would I be here now if I had? You can bet I'd not—I would have kept right on going afterwards—same as I would have run for it after I busted out of jail this morning. . . . Only I'm looking to straighten out this mess, not make a hunted man of myself."

Julie was staring at him intently. "You were in jail and broke out?"

Lake nodded. "Mayes, the storekeeper, and some others nailed me early this morning, threw me in a cell. Managed to get out while everybody was at the funerals for Dillow and the banker. Been trying to get here just about ever since."

95

The girl was silent as she looked down, studied her clenched hands. Finally, "What was it you wanted to ask me?"

He passed over the question now, discovering something of greater importance in his mind. "That mean you believe me? That I didn't shoot him?"

She stirred dispiritedly. "I—I don't know. Not sure what I think, but I want to believe you. Does seem, if you did, you'd not still be around."

Some of the tenseness faded from Lake Oliver. He nodded. "Exactly it. Had two chances to ride on, forget the whole thing—but I didn't take them. Not that I'm braver than anybody else. Fact is, I'm not. I'm pretty much of a coward when I think about going through life with a price on my head. That's why I want to get this all cleared up."

She managed a ghost of a smile. "I'll help if I can, Lake. What is it you want to know?"

Oliver got to his feet, stepped to the front window, and glanced out. The yard and the broad flat rolling out from the ranch were empty.

"Your pa's death—tell me just how it happened."

She wiped her lips nervously. "He was shot. From the side. He was on the way into town—"

"All right. Now—were you the first to meet him when he came back?"

Julie moved her head slightly. "I saw him come into the yard. He was leaning over—about to fall from the saddle. I was in here—I ran to him, helped him down."

"Did he say anything—speak any words?"

The girl bit at her lower lip. "I was so upset and frightened, I maybe didn't hear it all. And his voice was low, weak. I think he said: 'Sadilek. Get him, tell—' and then he just slumped in my arms. I turned to call Crucita after that."

96

" 'Sadilek. Get him, tell,' " Oliver repeated the words aloud thoughtfully as an earlier suspicion stirred through him again. "That's all you can remember?"

"There wasn't any more."

"You're dead sure that's the way he said it?"

Julie brushed at her eyes. "I—I think so. He was so weak I can't be certain."

"It mean anything to you?"

"Nothing. We know Mr. Sadilek, but he isn't a close friend."

"They didn't have a business deal or anything like that going, did they?"

"I'm sure they didn't. I would have known about it."

Lake rubbed absently at his paining leg. "Doesn't make much sense to me, does it to you?"

"Well, yes, I think it does. He just meant for me to get in touch with Mr. Sadilek—everybody figured he would be the marshal now that Rufe Dillow was dead—and tell him who it was that shot him. Only he died before he could give me the man's name."

"Probably the way it was," Lake admitted, "only I've been doing some wondering about this man Sadilek. He's the one around here who had the most to gain by the marshal's death—and he rides a bay horse, which seems to be a big thing in making folks believe I did it."

Julie was staring at him, a surprised look in her eyes. "You mean you think maybe Mr. Sadilek is the one who murdered my father—those others, too?"

"Not sure of anything, but for my money he's a good prospect."

The girl shook her head doubtfully. "I just don't

think so. I've—we've known him a long time. Not good friends, like I said, but we're well acquainted. He was always a nice man—honest, and folks liked him. He's not the kind who'd—"

"That's what I keep hearing, but you're all talking about the man Sadilek was, not what he maybe is now. Things happen that can cause changes. I'm a stranger to him, so I look at him without remembering how he used to be."

"Things?"

"Was told he'd sort of gone through his money. Investments he made didn't work out—and he was needing that job as marshal. Expect he was depending on it."

"And you think that because of that he could have been in on the bank robbery and the murders?"

"Not wondering so much about the holdup and the banker's killing. Some bunch just riding through could have pulled that—and he could have used them as a sort of a blind, make the marshal's death, and your pa's, look like they were all part of the same deal."

"But, my father—if what you say is true, why would Sadilek shoot him?"

"Sure can't answer that," Lake said, shrugging. "Would have to be on account of an accident. Your pa might have stumbled onto the truth and had to be shut up."

Julie stirred listlessly. "I don't know. Maybe you're right. . . . It's all so mixed up—so terrible."

"Just what it is," Oliver said, again stepping to the window.

She frowned. "Are you afraid someone followed you?"

"Not exactly. Had a little trouble in that grove

98

this side of town. Expect there'll be a posse dropping by here soon looking for me."

She came erect at once. "Then we'd best find a place for you to hide."

He smiled. "No, don't want that. You've had more than your share of grief."

"Then where will you go?"

"Into the hills again. Can find a place to lay low until I get this all figured out."

"What about food? You'll need—"

"Got enough to last a spell. If I can't get to the bottom of this mess in a couple of days, I figure to ride on to Canoncito, hand myself over to the law there, tell them the story. Maybe I can get a fair shake. Don't believe I can from this committee that runs San Sabal."

Alarm had filled her eyes. "But you can't be sure! They could just hand you over to the men here—believe you're guilty like they do."

"Chance I may have to take. That part about me being guilty—you don't think I am?"

She faced him squarely. "No . . . I guess I never really did."

Lake Oliver grinned broadly. "Means plenty to have you say that right out. Means I've for sure got to clear myself. . . . Now, reckon I'd best be getting out of here. You're liable to have company most any minute."

She nodded, then frowned, glanced down. "Your leg! I've watched you favor it. Shouldn't it be doctored?"

It's doing fine," he said, moving to the window.

She laid a hand on his arm. "When will I see you again?"

"Hard to say. Could be yet today or maybe tonight. And it could be a couple of days from now."

She leaned forward, kissed him lightly on the cheek, and stepped back. "I'll be waiting. . . . Take care."

"You can bet on it," he answered, and slipped through the window into the yard.

Chapter *FOURTEEN*

He could be certain there would be members of the posses in the area, possibly even then nearing the Carr ranch. For Julie's sake it was best he not be seen anywhere around.

Accordingly, he rode the bay straight west out of the yard, keeping close to the sheds and scrubby growth until he reached the arroyo that he once before had followed. He paused there; others would remember that he had taken that course, he realized. Immediately, then, he cut away from the wash, continued farther westward, thus placing himself well beyond the trail he had previously used.

Finally altering directions, he pointed the bay for a run of low hills to the south. He would be comparatively safe there for a time—at least long enough to think.

A short time later he came to a road, meeting it at right angles. A faded sign on a cedar post off to his right caught his attention, and he rode to it. *Canoncito 30 miles.* He remained motionless on the saddle, eyes riveted to the marker while that manner of solution to his troubles again presented itself.

It might be his best answer, but as Julie had pointed out, it could also prove to be only a matter of climbing from one pool of quicksand into another. He had no assurance that the law in Canoncito would see his position any different from the people of San Sabal. After a bit he shrugged; best he follow the course he had chosen, do his own snake skinning.

An hour later he reached the hills, which proved to be another line of bluffs, and selecting one of the higher red-faced formations, guided the bay to its flat crest and dismounted. The sun was hot but there was no growth large enough to offer shade, so he could do nothing but locate a level place where no rocks studded the soil and stretch out.

The dull ache in his leg eased at once when he took his weight off it, and mopping away the sweat on his brow and tipping his hat forward over his eyes, he fell to reviewing the information he had turned up by talking with Julie Carr and the saloonman, McCoy.

All lumped together, it still helped very little, he had to admit, but somewhere there was a key to the puzzle if he could only find it. Finally, after threshing it about in his mind, he went back to the start, considered the incidents as he knew them, taking them step by step.

Four men robbed a bank, killed the banker, Hilton, in the process. One of the outlaws had been riding a bay horse and according to Deputy Cal Jessup, looked very much like him—so much so, in fact, that he was ready to testify to the identification.

Then came the posses, several of them. He had been jumped by one whose leader had been the town marshal, Rufe Dillow. He had managed to escape the lawman and his party, taking a bullet in his leg in the effort. While he was riding on seeking help, someone had shot Dillow in the back during the search that had ensued. No one had gotten a glimpse of the killer, but all assumed it to be him.

There was nothing to indicate that the man seen fleeing the bank on a bay horse after the killing and robbery was the same as the one who had slain Rufe Dillow. But by the same logic, there was no reason not to believe it, either.

Next followed the bushwhacking of Ben Carr. No one saw the murderer, so again there was no way of knowing if it was the same man striking for the third time. Likely it was—except there was no need for Ben Carr's death, unless, as Lake had thought earlier, the rancher had discovered by sheer accident the identity of the killer.

Sadilek. Get him, tell. . . .

Oliver's thoughts came to a halt as he recalled the rancher's last words. Could he—and Julie—be misinterpreting them? Instead of endeavoring to convey instructions to the girl as she believed, was he trying to say something else? Could he have meant that Sadilek was his murderer, that she was to tell someone—possibly Deputy Marshal Jessup—of the fact?

Get him could mean just what it said, and words substituted to complete the faltering sentence would work out to say: *Sadilek—get him. . . . He is the killer. . . . Tell Cal Jessup.*

It made sense, and it fit in with Lake Oliver's suspicions. He was seeing Russ Sadilek in an entirely different light from McCoy and Julie and others who had known the man through the years. As a stranger he could take an impartial, uninfluenced view of the man; there was no preconceived conception built up through the years that declared he was incapable of crime.

Too, there was an odd thing; what had happened to the outlaws who had robbed the bank and murdered Hilton? With the large number of posse riders out almost at once combing the country—why had none of them been caught or at least seen?

True, thanks to Rufe Dillow's one-track mind, the concentration had been on him, and such could have bearing on the posses' failure to overhaul the bandits, but it wasn't reasonable to believe that no one had gotten at least a glimpse of the renegades.

That seemed to lead to but one conclusion: the four men who had been involved were still around, were likely hiding nearby—probably right in town. If so, they had outside help; someone had furnished them with a place to hole up where they could remain until the excitement died off, which would occur when another man paid the penalty for what they had done. . . . And that other man was him.

That thought sobered Lake Oliver, brought a grimness to his eyes. He swiped at the sweat on his face with a forearm, stared off across the hills and flats below. Far over in the direction of San Sabal three riders moved slowly in the streaming sunlight. . . . Posse members. . . . They were hunting him everywhere. Even the far south buttes where he presently was soon would become unsafe, and he would need to find another place in which to lie low while he struggled to get the answers that would clear him.

But he couldn't keep running, hiding, dodging the posses. As well give it up, move on, get entirely out of the San Sabal hills. It would add up to the same result—a hunted man there as well as elsewhere in the country.

Yet, how could he shift the blame from his shoulders to those of the guilty man? Who was he?

He had only a hunch that Russ Sadilek was the killer—a hunch that both Julie and Tom McCoy discounted, and that likely everyone else in the valley would also deny.

But it was logical to him. All he needed was a way to prove it—a means, a trick perhaps, that would induce the murderer to tip his hand and reveal himself.

How?

Restless, irritated by his own failure to find a solution, Lake Oliver rose, made his way to the rim of the bluff. Below him a colony of prairie dogs moved about, trotting back and forth from one mound to another, now and then chiding each other sharply with shrill barks. Despite enemies at every hand—the birds of prey, the larger snakes, and other animals, particularly coyotes—the doughty little rodents managed to thrive. If ever they—

Oliver's mind halted on dead center. The ruse employed by coyotes to capture prairie dogs came to him suddenly. The lean, shaggy brothers to the wolf hunted in pairs. While one lay hidden close to the mounds, the other would walk through the colony, sending the dogs scurrying into their burrows, from which they watched in safety until their enemy, plainly visible, had vanished into the distance.

Reassured, they would then reappear, whereupon the coyote in hiding would spring upon the nearest and make the kill.

A hard smile cracked Oliver's mouth. That was the answer—a decoy. Force Sadilek to show himself. But he couldn't pull it off alone; he'd need someone to work with, someone he could trust. Julie Carr was the logical choice. She needed only to pass the word along that she had recalled more of what her father had said before he died, information that would point to the killer. Such would have the desired effect—but he couldn't use Julie. It would be dangerous, and he was reluctant to subject her to any risk.

Someone else—Tom McCoy. . . . The saloonman would serve the purpose. Lake nodded in satisfaction. He'd hold off until dark when it was safer to move, and then return to the settlement. He was sure McCoy would agree to the plan he'd outline to him.

Chapter *FIFTEEN*

At full dark Lake Oliver rode down from the buttes and halted in the trees west of San Sabal. He dismounted there, leaving the bay on a tether, and proceeded to the rear of the White Eagle Saloon on foot.

The gelding would be far from handy at such distance, but Lake figured that it no longer mattered. If his plan failed he would be at the mercy of the town and he'd have no use for a horse. At the moment the important thing was not to be seen entering McCoy's.

Avoiding the yard with the dog where the old man had grumpily challenged his passage that morning, he gained the alley behind the saloon and adjacent buildings on that side of the street. Lamps had been lit and a yellow dust-trapped glare hung over the settlement like a pale canopy, turning back the glow and muting the sounds that were rising.

San Sabal was still in a fever of turbulence over the murders, and it had been further heightened by his encounter with Harry Gibbs and the man called Anse. But the posses would have returned with sunset and likely were now relating their experiences and laying plans to start the search again that coming morning.

There could be a change there, Lake thought as he slipped quietly through the shadows to the window of Tom McCoy's office; it was possible there'd be no need for a further probing of the hills and flats if all went well. A wry grin tugged at his lips. The failure of his scheme would have the same result; he would be their prisoner.

Pulling up close to the wall of the building, he peered through the dusty square of glass. The room was empty. McCoy was probably in behind his bar helping to serve customers, or elsewhere about the place. Lake guessed it was just as well that the man was away from his office at the moment.

Stepping back, Lake moved to the side entrance. Directly ahead of him at the end of the passage way two men had halted, were in conversation. Beyond them he could see strollers idling along the walks. Music, rising from a saloon somewhere farther down, hung faintly in the warm, still air, and a woman's laugh, soft and pleasant, came to him from a second-floor window of the nearby building.

Laying his hand on the knob, he tried the door. It gave readily, and throwing his glance again to the ends of the narrow space to be certain he was not seen, he entered.

A surge of confused sounds and hot air heavy with mingled odors struck him as he stepped hurriedly into the room. Closing the door quickly, he moved in behind the coatrack, unchanged from where he had placed it, and leaned against the wall.

He didn't think it probable, but there was that chance someone in the saloon looking into McCoy's office at that exact moment had seen him enter. If so, he would be ready for any reaction. Breathing slowly, he remained in the shelter of the rack for three or four minutes, and then when no one appeared in the doorway, reckoned his arrival had gone unnoticed, and settled back to wait for McCoy.

Time, filled with the noises of the saloon—laughter, talk, an occasional crash as a chair tipped over or a glass was knocked to the floor; the half-hearted thumping on a piano, the high tremolo of a tenor voice rendering a plaintive ballad of thwarted love—passed, became a half hour, an hour.

Oliver, leg paining him, weary of waiting, of standing, swore feelingly. He hadn't counted on delay. His plan depended upon getting word passed to the largest number of persons, if it was to be effective.

His attention paused on the open door. Perhaps, closed, it would draw Tom McCoy's eye. Edging forward, he put his left hand against the flimsy panel, eased it shut. The volume of racket decreased somewhat, and the office, deprived of light, fell into darkness.

He hadn't considered that. Digging into a pocket Lake produced a match, thumbed it into life, and crossing to the lamp on McCoy's desk, touched the wick. A small square of flame sprang up, and taking the knob, he set it to proper level. He moved then to the window, drew the blind; he wanted no outsiders looking in while he spoke with the saloon-man.

There was a sound of heavy steps at the door. The idea had worked exactly as he had hoped—assuming it was McCoy coming to investigate. Lake took no chance, stepped in behind the coatrack, pistol in hand.

A moment later the tension eased. It was the

saloonman, collar off, sweat beading his forehead, a frown on his face.

"Close it," Oliver said, coming into the center of the room.

McCoy's eyes flared with surprise. He threw a hasty glance into the saloon, and then, stepping to one side, pushed the door shut.

"You loco? Every man in town's out there—"

Lake nodded. "What I was hoping for."

McCoy, puzzled, stared at him. "Then you're more than loco. Feeling's running ten times stronger against you now than this morning—what with your caving in Joe Anse's head and planting a bullet in Gibbs's shoulder."

"Tried to keep from doing that. Didn't want to shoot it out with anybody but they gave me no choice. Man's got a right to stay alive—and I wasn't about to let them take me—especially Gibbs."

"Why him?"

"If he'd had his way I'd be swinging in the wind right now. Seems he was a friend of Ben Carr— but that's not important. Think I've figured out a way to trap the real killer and get this town off my back."

McCoy sank into a chair. "You know who it is?"

"Got a good idea—Sadilek."

"Sadilek! You were talking about him this morning. Thought we decided he's not likely to be the one."

"Was a few things I learned from Julie—Julie Carr. Adding them to the way things have shaped up makes me think all the more that he's—"

"Think!" McCoy cut in. "Hell, you've got to have proof if you're going to pin it on him."

"Know that, and I've worked up a way to get it if you'll help."

The saloonman shifted nervously, looked toward the closed door, seemingly listening to the sounds beyond it. Finally he shook his head.

"Not so sure I ought to get mixed up in a deal like this—no more'n I already am, anyway. I live in this town, depend on folks here to keep my business going. Just can't afford to get all crossways."

"You won't," Oliver said quietly. "All you've got to do is go out there, drop the word confidential like to your bartender that you know who the killer is."

McCoy rose to his feet slowly. "You want me to what?" he demanded in an incredulous voice.

"You heard it right. Got to start the rumor that you know who the murderer is, and there's no better place to plant it than with a bartender.

"Want you to tell him that I found out, told you so's I could clear myself, then rode on to Arizona, and that you're going back in your office and get off a letter to the U.S. Marshal in Santa Fe so's he can come and take over."

Tom McCoy realized the implications of the scheme at once. "Sets me up like a duck in a shooting gallery. Guess you know that."

Lake nodded. "That's why I'll be waiting here behind this rack ready for Sadilek when he comes in to stop you from sending word to the marshal."

The saloonman thought for a moment. Then: "One big hole in your figuring; we've got a deputy here. He's the one who ought to be told, not me."

"Thought of that. I couldn't get within talking distance of Jessup without getting filled full of lead —not after breaking jail this morning, and shooting Harry Gibbs."

McCoy said, "That'll make sense, but here's another thing—why call in the U.S. Marshal? Why not let Cal arrest the killer?"

"Can't see your bartender asking any questions like that one, but if he does just say that I don't trust the deputy, that I made you give me your word you'd turn it over to a federal lawman."

Again the storekeeper was lost in thought. After a bit he looked up, smiled. "Well, when you want me to get things going?"

Lake Oliver sighed with relief. At last he was beginning to get somewhere. "Right now. You start the rumor, it'll spread fast. Ought to get some action in a hurry."

"No doubt. . . . Only hope I'll be alive to know about it."

"You'll be alive," Oliver said firmly. "I can guarantee that."

The saloonman studied Lake briefly. "Yeh, reckon you can," he said. "Now, want to be sure I've got this straight. I pass the word to the bartender that I've just talked to you—"

"This door being closed ought to back that."

"For a fact. Never close it unless I've got private business. Anyway, I say you found out who the killer is and told me, made me promise to send for the U.S. Marshal right away and turn the information over to him."

Lake Oliver nodded. "And that I rode on. Had to get to Arizona—got a job waiting for me there and I didn't want any truck with this town."

"Then I come back in here, shut the door like I was writing the letter to the marshal."

"All there is to it. Once you're in here, we set tight—and wait until either that door or the one letting out into the passageway opens and Sadilek steps in."

"If he's the one," McCoy murmured, glance on the side entrance. "Not so sure about that door. Man could throw it open, shoot from outside. I'd be dead before you could step in."

"Can fix that quick.. I'll shove this rack over to that side of the room. That way it'll block you off and give me a chance to watch both doors."

"That'll handle it all right," the saloonman said, and smiled. "Well, here goes. You realize if this don't pan out like you think, you're in a jackpot for sure. You'll never get out of this town alive."

"Chance I've got to take."

"Fair enough," McCoy said, and waiting until Lake had stationed himself behind the rack out of sight, crossed the room and entered the saloon.

Chapter *SIXTEEN*

Alone, Lake Oliver leaned against the wall. He drew his pistol, checked the loads. He'd use it on the killer if forced, but he was hoping it would not be necessary. Better to let the law—the town's committee—dole out the punishment. *Another chore for the hangmen of San Sabel,* he thought, and then a hard grin tugged at his lips. If his plan went wrong he very likely would be the object of the committee's attention.

It was hot in McCoy's office. With both doors shut, the window closed, the air lay trapped and unmoving. Lake brushed at the sweat misting his eyes, shifted uncomfortably. Likely he was taking unnecessary precautions, standing ready now for the killer. Chances were Russ Sadilek wouldn't make his move for some time after McCoy returned, supposedly to pen a letter to the marshal in Santa Fe. He should figure at least an hour for the word to get around. But Lake felt he could not afford to gamble. He'd best be ready each and every moment until the killer was safely behind bars.

The racket within the saloon seemed to be increasing. Normal, Oliver decided, since the night was young and the crowd was still gathering. There was a crash as something fell to the floor, a yell, and then laughter. Someone had tripped probably, either accidentally or victim of a practical joker. The plinking of the piano paused briefly at the confusion, then resumed.

His thoughts shifted to Julie Carr, to the job that did await him in Arizona. He wondered if he dared ask her to go with him, to help build the ranch that had occupied his dreams. He didn't have much to offer a woman—a past that was a detriment, a future that was a slim one at best.

She'd be a fool to accept. She had a ranch of her own—a good house and all the necessary things that made for comfort and fine living and little worry. To ask her to give it up would be unfair. He frowned, rubbed at his jaw as a different speculation came to him. What if she asked him to stay, to help her, to become a part of the life she had? Could he give up his own plans?

He grinned then, shook off all such contemplation. He was a long way from being in a position to make any decisions—either way. He was still the object of a determined manhunt, and until he cleared himself of all charges concerning that, he'd best not think about the future. But there—

Abruptly the door opened. Lake Oliver drew up sharply, relaxed when he saw that it was McCoy. The saloonman glanced at him, nodded as he closed the panel and crossed to the table he used as a desk.

"Got it going," he said, sinking into his chair. "Hope it works—for your sake."

"Better, or I'm cooked. How'd the bartender take it?"

"Swallowed it whole. I stalled around a bit afterwards, watched him drop the word. Could see those he told walk off and get into little groups. I made a

115

special point of telling him I wanted it kept quiet—and that I wasn't to be bothered while I was writing the letter. Even said for him to keep an eye out for Ed Pringle—he's the one that rides messenger for folks around here."

McCoy had made a good job of it. Oliver nodded his satisfaction. "Sadilek out there?"

"Yeh, setting in a card game with Jessup and some others. The deputy's nursing that wallop you handed him this morning. Killing off the pain with a bottle."

"Good thing we're not depending on him for any help. . . . Might just be smart to send for the U.S. Marshal, let him take over if—"

Lake's words cut short as a light rap sounded at the side door. He came about swiftly, silently, wincing as the twist sent pain shooting through his leg, brought his pistol to bear on the entrance. A moment later the panel swung in.

It was Cal Jessup.

Oliver swore, settled back. The lawman had taken it on himself to horn in. "Smart thing for you to do is—"

"Hand over that gun," the deputy said in a cold voice.

Lake stiffened. A stride away Tom McCoy came to his feet, disbelief on his face.

"You—was you!"

"Yeh—was me."

Jessup's expression changed slightly. "Keep standing there, Tom. Don't make no bad moves or try yelling unless you want me to blow your friend's head off."

Oliver passed his weapon to Jessup slowly, his own amazement matched that of the saloonman. He hadn't once suspected the deputy, had stubbornly

116

stuck to his conviction that it was Russ Sadilek. He'd been wrong all the way.

The lawman thrust the pistol under his waistband, jerked his head at McCoy. He had removed the bandage Lake had noted earlier, and the welt left by the cartridge belt was an ugly purple.

"Now we're taking a little walk—over to my place."

The saloonkeeper frowned. "Your house? Why?"

"Got some friends holed up there. Aim to let them boys take the pair of you out to the brakes—"

"Boys," Oliver repeated. "You mean the bunch that robbed the bank and killed Hilton?"

Cal Jessup shrugged, took a step to one side and allowed McCoy to move in next to Lake. "The old man was a damned fool. . . . Tried to put up a fight."

"Then it was you that shot the Marshal and Ben Carr?"

"Your guessing's pretty good, but it ain't going to help you much. Rufe got wise somehow, and old Ben seen me carrying a lot of grub into my house that night after the bank robbery. Reckon he got to thinking about it later, him knowing I lived alone and done my eating in town.

"When I run into him out there on the trail I could see he had it all figured out and was heading for town to do some talking. Could tell from the way he acted. Was nothing I could do but shut him up."

Jessup edged up to McCoy's desk, reached for the sheet of paper the saloonman had laid out. He picked it up, scanned its surface. It was blank.

"This here the letter you was sending to the marshal?"

McCoy nodded, smiled wryly. "Funny thing—you ain't the man we set the trap for."

Jessup's eyes narrowed as he moved toward the side door. "What's that mean?"

"Wasn't you we figured would come."

The deputy halted, one hand on the knob, the other holding his cocked pistol, leveled at the two men.

"You saying you didn't know it was me?"

Lake Oliver, tense, searching for a way to distract the lawman, recover his own weapon before it was too late, shrugged. "Never suspected you at all, Deputy. If you hadn't showed up, we'd never known," he said, and took an offhand step toward the coatrack. . . . If he could get to it, lunge against its end and drive it into the man—

"Easy!" Jessup barked, bringing his gun to bear directly on Lake.

Oliver froze. The deputy hung there rigid for a long moment, and then his shoulders relented slightly. "Reckon I should've held off," he murmured.

"For sure," McCoy said. "Overplayed your hand this time."

"Maybe, but you're the ones that'll be paying. Cat's out of the bag now. Means I'll just have to go ahead. . . . Out that door—careful and quiet."

"Going to be hard explaining my killing—Oliver's too, far as that goes," McCoy said, stalling. Evidently he was hoping someone would come through from the saloon despite the instructions he had left that no one was to disturb him.

"Won't be no need to explain nothing. Boys'll take you out to the brakes while I trot myself back, show up on the street—and in your place. Folks will think I been there all the time."

118

"Then tomorrow somebody'll find us, figure we shot each other."

"Don't make no difference what they think. You both'll be dead, and I'll be in the clear. . . . Move out."

McCoy drew back. Beads of sweat stood out on his forehead and his face had turned chalk-white. "Now, wait a minute, Cal! You can't—"

"Move!" the deputy snarled, and wagged his pistol at Lake. "You first. McCoy'll be right behind you—and I'll be right behind him with my gun aimed at his head. You take one wrong step and he's dead—savvy?"

Oliver nodded. His brain was still working fast, frantically searching for a way to save the saloon-man and himself from death at the hands of Jessup's outlaws, but there seemed little hope at that moment. Perhaps out in the open, in the passageway, it would be possible to attract someone's attention—

"Go down to the alley, turn right. House you'll see at the end—that's my place. It's where we're going first."

Silent, Lake Oliver stepped through the door-way.

119

Chapter *SEVENTEEN*

The passageway was dark as Oliver, at the head of the short procession, moved into it. A short distance away the street stirred with milling persons strolling aimlessly about soaking in the night's coolness. They would be unaware of what was taking place; to them the narrow space between the two buildings was a black void.

Walking slowly, favoring his leg, eyes switching back and forth as he sought help, Oliver continued toward the alley. Close on his heels he could hear Tom McCoy; the saloonman's strained breathing was clearly audible.

They came to the area back of the buildings. Hope stirred anew in Lake. There might be someone in the alley or loitering behind one of the structures. . . . If so, he'd try to attract their attention without alerting Jessup. . . . But the narrow, dusty strip was empty as the passageway, the landing deserted.

Grim, he cut right as the deputy had directed, centered his attention on a house at the end of the settlement, a good hundred yards away. He had that much time and space in which to come up with something.

It would have to be quick and sure, a move that would take Cal Jessup by surprise. The deputy would kill the saloonman instantly unless prevented. The lawman had nothing to lose, and he could easily explain the deaths of McCoy and Lake by saying he had encountered them moving down the alley, that McCoy was a prisoner of the man all suspected had committed the murders.

Jessup would say that in the ensuing shoot-out the saloonkeeper had been downed by the killer, who in turn had been shot by him. Such would be a contradiction of the rumor that had circulated through town earlier—but that had been no more than that—a rumor. Here was proof—here was the killer, the man everyone knew had committed the crimes that had stirred up San Sabal.

Lake shrugged helplessly. He couldn't risk Tom McCoy's life. . . . Jessup held all the high cards.

The house loomed up directly ahead, dark and foreboding. If the four men who had aided in the bank robbery and the killing of Hilton were inside, they had the windows covered to mask any lamps that were burning.

"Easy now," the deputy warned as they turned into the yard. "Don't try nothing."

Lake proceeded haltingly up the narrow path between the weeds to the door, and halted. He half turned, McCoy beside him.

"Knock—three times," Cal Jessup ordered.

Oliver shook his head. "The hell with you," he said flatly. "If you think I'm going to help you kill me, you're loco."

Jessup grinned into the half dark, edged by the two men. Lifting a hand, he gave the specified signal, stepped back. The moments dragged. The lawman, anger stiffening him, rapped again. A chair

121

scraped against the floor inside. Boot heels sounded.

"Cal?" a low voice called.

"Open the goddam door!" the deputy snapped irritably. "Hurry it up!"

A key grated in a lock. Jessup started to fall back, permit his prisoners to step up onto the narrow landing, enter. For a brief instant he was turned away.

In that fragment of time Lake Oliver reacted. He lunged forward. His fingers wrapped about the deputy's arm. Ignoring the pain in his leg, he pivoted, put all his strength and weight into the movement, and swung Jessup at the door.

The gun in the lawman's hand blasted as he crashed head-on into the panel, splintering it from its hinges. It drove into the man caught in the act of opening it, smashed him to the floor. A yell went up from him, was echoed by someone else inside.

Lake, bending forward hurriedly, scooped up the weapon dropped by the stunned deputy, triggered a shot at a figure rushing up to the doorway, fired again at a stab of flame that spurted from the black interior of the house.

He dropped to hands and knees, worked up close to the entrance, looking, listening for the others. An arm's length away Tom McCoy was slamming a fist into Cal Jessup's jaw, preventing him from rising.

"You—inside!" Oliver called. "Place's covered. Come out with your hands up high—or you're dead."

Silence hung for a brief time, punctuated by the groans of the two men sprawled in the doorway. Finally a voice responded.

"Where's Jessup?"

"He can't do you or himself any good," Oliver answered. "You've got about ten seconds left."

"We're coming," the voice said immediately.

Lake got to his feet, took up a stand at the edge of the doorway as McCoy dragged the unconscious Jessup to one side. Boots were pounding along the alley and men were shouting back and forth. The gunshots had been heard on the street.

"Throw your guns out first."

Two distinct thuds on the landing followed. Lake, extending a foot, kicked the weapons off into the weeds.

"All right, come on."

Men were crowding into the yard. Lake heard Sadilek put a question to Tom McCoy, who answered briefly, concisely, but he was only half listening while he waited for the two outlaws to step into the open.

Someone said: "Then it weren't him a'tall? Was Jessup?"

"Him and these four jaspers," the saloonman said. "There's two laying there where Oliver downed them, and two more coming out."

Lake hustled the pair up against the wall of the house. "Keep reaching," he said coldly, and came around to face the crowd packing the yard. Jessup was still prone, and someone had provided a length of cord and was lashing the deputy's wrists together.

Oliver singled out Russ Sadilek. "Had you pegged wrong. I'm begging your pardon for that."

The tall man frowned. "Don't know what you mean—"

"I'll do the explaining later," McCoy cut in. "Think we're the ones who ought to be apologizing to this man after what the town's done to him."

"No doubt of that," Sadilek said, still puzzled

123

by Lake's words. "I'll say it for all of us now; we were wrong. If there's anything we can do to make it right, speak up."

"Call it even," Lake said, giving McCoy a smile of thanks. "I'm bearing no grudge."

"Then maybe you'd be interested in hanging around, maybe taking on the deputy marshal's job." It was Mayes, the storekeeper. "Russ'll be needing some good help."

Oliver shook his head. "Obliged, but I got other things in mind," he said, sliding his gun back into its holster. He could have explained that he was due at the Carr ranch, that he had important matters to discuss with Julie, and decisions to make, but he only turned away and started up the path to the street.

"So long," he called back. "Could be I'll see you later."

Ray Hogan is an author who has inspired a loyal following over the years since he published his first Western novel *Ex-marshal* in 1956. Hogan was born in Willow Springs, Missouri, where his father was town marshal. At five the Hogan family moved to Albuquerque where Ray Hogan still lives in the foothills of the Sandia and Manzano mountains. His father was on the Albuquerque police force and, in later years, owned the Overland Hotel. It was while listening to his father and other old-timers tell tales from the past that Ray was inspired to recast these tales in fiction. From the beginning he did exhaustive research into the history and the people of the Old West and the walls of his study are lined with various firearms, spurs, pictures, books, and memorabilia, about all of which he can talk in dramatic detail. Among his most popular works are the series of books about Shawn Starbuck, a searcher in a quest for a lost brother, who has a clear sense of right and wrong and who is willing to stand up and be counted when it is a question of fairness or justice. His other major series is about lawman John Rye whose reputation has earned him the sobriquet The Doomsday Marshal. 'I've attempted to capture the courage and bravery of those men and women that lived out West and the dangers and problems they had to overcome,' Hogan once remarked. If his lawmen protagonists seem sometimes larger than life, it is because they are men of integrity, heroes who through grit of character and common sense are able to overcome the obstacles they encounter despite often overwhelming odds. This same grit of character can also be found in Hogan's heroines and, in *The Vengeance of Fortuna West*, Hogan wrote a gripping and totally believable account of a woman who takes up the badge and tracks the men who killed her lawman husband by ambush. No less intriguing in her way is Nellie Dupray, convicted of rustling in *The Glory Trail*. Above all, what is most impressive about Hogan's Western novels is the consistent quality with which each is crafted, the compelling depth of his characters, and his ability to juxtapose the complexities of human conflict into narratives always as intensely interesting as they are emotionally involving. His latest novel is *Soldier in Buckskin*.